POISON PEN

Tanya Landman is the author of many books for children, including *Waking Merlin* and *Merlin's Apprentice*, *The World's Bellybutton* and *The Kraken Snores*, *Sam Swann's Movie Mysteries: Zombie Dawn!!!* and three stories featuring the characters Flotsam and Jetsam. Of *Poison Pen*, the seventh title in her award-winning Poppy Fields series, Tanya says, "When the first Poppy Fields book was published I was sent off on a promotional tour and had great fun devising murder plots from the eye-poppingly gruesome suggestions from the audience. It occurred to me later that a book festival – with envious undercurrents and hidden tensions – would be a perfect setting for another mystery."

Tanya is also the author of two novels for teenagers: *Apache*, which was shortlisted for the Carnegie Medal and the Booktrust Teenage Fiction Prize, and *The Goldsmith's Daughter*, which was nominated for the Guardian Children's Fiction Prize. Since 1992, Tanya has also been part of Storybox Theatre. She lives with her family in Devon.

You can find out more about Tanya Landman
and her books by visiting her website at
www.tanyalandman.com

Poppy Fields is on the case!

Mondays are Murder
Dead Funny
Dying to be Famous
The Head is Dead
The Scent of Blood
Certain Death
Poison Pen
Love Him to Death
Blood Hound
The Will to Live

Also by Tanya Landman

Sam Swann's Movie Mysteries: Zombie Dawn!!!
Waking Merlin
Merlin's Apprentice
The World's Bellybutton
The Kraken Snores

For younger readers

Flotsam and Jetsam
Flotsam and Jetsam and the Stormy Surprise
Flotsam and Jetsam and the Grooof
Mary's Penny

For older readers

Apache
The Goldsmith's Daughter

POISON PEN

TANYA LANDMAN

WALKER
BOOKS

First published 2010 by Walker Books Ltd
87 Vauxhall Walk, London SE11 5HJ

This edition published 2013

2 4 6 8 10 9 7 5 3 1

Text © 2010 Tanya Landman
Cover illustration © 2013 Scott Garrett

The right of Tanya Landman to be identified as author of this work has been asserted by her in accordance with the Copyright, Designs and Patents Act 1988

This book has been typeset in Slimbach

Printed and bound in Great Britain by Clays Ltd, St Ives plc

British Library Cataloguing in Publication Data:
a catalogue record for this book is available from the British Library

ISBN 978-1-4063-4778-4

www.walker.co.uk

For Daniel, John and every cherub-faced child I've met who's possessed by a gruesome imagination...

BY *7 p.m. the London offices of Fletcher, Beaumont & Grimm were almost deserted. Almost, but not quite. In a book-lined study a reader sat behind a mahogany desk, turning the pages of a freshly typed manuscript. The silence was broken only by the occasional rustling of paper and the steady ticking of a grandfather clock. Across the room a leather armchair creaked as Sebastian Vincent, the manuscript's author, shifted nervously, waiting for the reader's response.*

At last the wait was over. Sebastian watched as the final page was replaced carefully and smoothed with a sigh of satisfaction. That was a good sign, wasn't it? He hoped so, after the blood, sweat and tears he had put into writing it!

The reader met his eye and nodded before saying, "This is a work of rare genius, Mr Vincent. Very many congratulations."

Sebastian gulped. "You think you'll publish it?"

"Oh yes. I will have to present it for approval at our next editorial meeting, but that's a mere formality. Your book is thrilling. Unputdownable, as they say. There's no doubt in my mind that you have a prize-winner here – a bestseller." There was a pause and the reader's

eyes narrowed a fraction. "Tell me, Mr Vincent... Have you shown your book to anyone else? Any other publishers, for example? To anyone at all?"

Sebastian shook his head. It was true. He hadn't shown it to anyone in the book world, at any rate. "I came straight to Fletcher, Beaumont & Grimm. I'd heard you were the best, you see."

"Good. Very good." The reader smiled and threw open the door of a well-stocked drinks cabinet. "Can I get you something?"

Sebastian looked uncomfortable. "I can't. I'm on medication, you see." He let out an awkward laugh. "A drink would be fatal!"

"Well, maybe an orange juice, then?"

"Thank you."

Sebastian's mind was dancing with glorious images: book signings with queues of adoring fans; literary festivals with eager readers hanging on his every word; TV and radio programmes with respectful critics asking for his opinion on the issues of the day. He swallowed his juice, not noticing its strangely bitter aftertaste, and then stood up to leave.

Still dreaming of a golden future, he shook the reader's hand warmly. Sebastian smiled, and the grin didn't leave his face as he was escorted through the maze of corridors to the front entrance. The moment the reader closed the door behind him, Sebastian pulled out his mobile and tapped in a number. He couldn't wait to relay the good news.

"Well? What did they say?" demanded a voice at the other end of the phone. "Did they like it?"

Sebastian didn't answer. He was suddenly doubled up with pain. He yelped. Gasped. Moaned. The phone fell from his hand.

"Sebastian? Seb? What's happening?" The voice was shrill with panic. "Say something! Are you all right?"

Sebastian Vincent was as far from all right as it was possible for anyone to be. He writhed and convulsed, screaming – begging – for the pain to stop. And thirty seconds later it did. Thirty seconds later he was perfectly still.

Thirty seconds later Sebastian Vincent was curled on the pavement. Dead.

GOOD READS

MY name is Poppy Fields. When my friend Graham and I volunteered to help out at the local book festival, our school librarian told us it would "really make things come alive". She solemnly swore that meeting authors would be exciting; that their characters would "come leaping off the page".

She didn't mean it literally.

But on the very first morning, a fictional being really did seem to spring out of a book. Weirder still, he appeared to have Evil Intentions towards his creator. Before long, authors were getting attacked left, right and centre – and Graham and I found ourselves slap-bang in the middle of another murder investigation.

We have Book Week at school every year and it's normally a low-key sort of affair. Mrs Woodward, the librarian, puts up a few extra posters and the English department drags in a not-very-well-known author or poet to give creative writing sessions. It's not what you'd call mind-blowingly thrilling stuff, and I wouldn't have put meeting real live writers on my 10 Things To Do Before I Die list. But the idea of getting involved in the book festival was irresistible: Viola Boulder made sure of that.

Viola was the organizer of the brand new Good Reads Festival. She'd persuaded a load of well-known authors (and a whole bunch of lesser-known ones) to come to our town for an action-packed weekend of events. There were going to be Seriously Earnest talks for grown-ups, but she'd planned a load of fun stuff too: storytimes for the tiddly-tots and write-your-own-horror workshops for teenagers. When Mrs Woodward announced the whole thing in assembly, she was almost quivering with excitement.

"It's a wonderful opportunity to meet first-class writers like Francisco Botticelli—"

She was interrupted by a small explosion of enthusiasm from the fantasy-lovers in the hall. Francisco Botticelli writes seriously long epics about dragons and trolls. You know the sort of stuff: innocent young boy must fight the forces of evil aided by a fire-breathing dragon and a few trusty gnomes. The baddie is supposed to be all-powerful but, surprise, surprise, after a few tearful death scenes with minor characters, the goodies win against overwhelming odds and everything's fine until the next bumper volume comes along. His new one was called *Dragons and Demons* and it ran to a whopping 786 pages. Francisco Botticelli's books are massive in every sense. Personally, I think they're a health hazard. You wouldn't want to read one in bed. I mean, if you fell asleep holding it, you could give yourself a nasty head injury.

Once the murmuring had died down, Mrs Woodward spoke again. "Another author I'm sure you'll be looking forward to seeing is ... Katie Bell."

This time there was an outbreak of gasps and sighs. Katie Bell wrote pink, spangly books about LURVE. As far as I can see, they all have pretty much the same storyline: girl meets boy and they fall deeply in lurve, then girl and boy have argument and, after a lot of weeping and several boxes of tissues, girl and boy get back together for ever. Her current book was called *Stupid Cupid* and the cover had a heart with an arrow through the middle. I can't quite see the fascination myself, but I reckon at least half the girls in school worship Katie Bell.

The librarian went on to explain that the opening event would be with Charlie Deadlock, author not only of the supremely popular football series featuring Sam the Striker, but also of *The Spy Complex*, a new novel that was hotly tipped to win prizes. Muriel Black, the author of *Wizard Wheezes*, a book about – you've guessed it – a mischievous group of young wizards at boarding school, would be doing an event on the Saturday. So would Basil Tamworth, who wrote pig tales like *This Boar's Life*, involving Farmer Biggins and his herd of Gloucester Old Spots, all of which manage to miraculously avoid the usual porcine fate of being turned into sausages.

And, as if all that wasn't enough, Mrs Woodward told us that Zenith would be there. There was a spontaneous outburst of singing and pelvic thrusting at the back of the hall. Zenith had been a rock star who'd had loads of number one hits with outrageously raunchy songs like *Do It Now* and *Do It Again* and *Do It One More Time*. She'd made the kind of pop videos that were embarrassing to watch if your gran was in the room. But then she'd adopted several children and gone weirdly spiritual: she was now a vegan who ate only pulses and drank only rainwater. She was getting pretty old. She'd had so many facelifts that her real eyebrows had disappeared into her hairline and she had to crayon on replacements. Zenith had written a book called *Princess Peony and her Perfect Pony Petrushka*. The cover was heavily pink, with lashings of sparkles. As Mrs Woodward said Zenith's name, she sniffed as if she didn't approve of either the singer or the book.

Then the librarian topped everything by announcing the festival's Grand Finale. She was bursting with pride as she said, "I've saved the biggest name for last. Has anyone heard of Esmerelda Desiree?"

Screams. Roars. Whooping and cheering. A deafening outbreak of applause. Esmerelda Desiree. Glamorous author of the blockbuster, gazillion-bestselling *The Vampiress of Venezia*, which had recently been turned into a box-office-record-breaking movie. The woman was mega-famous. You'd have to have spent the last two years sitting under a stone, blindfolded and with extremely effective ear plugs, *not* to have heard of her.

Eventually, once the noise had died down enough for her to speak, Mrs Woodward revealed the reason for announcing the Good Reads Festival highlights. Viola Boulder wanted ten volunteers – student ambassadors, she called them – to help with the events.

"Anyone interested can come and put their name down at breaktime. It will be on a strictly first come, first served basis. And for those of you who aren't able to volunteer or to attend the festival, don't worry. I'll make sure I obtain signed copies of the authors' books for the school library."

To be honest, I wasn't an especially big fan of any of the writers she'd mentioned, but I was dead keen to meet them in the flesh. I mean, they had to be a pretty weird bunch. They must spend all day on their own dreaming up imaginary worlds – it's not like a proper grown-up job, is it? I'm interested in human behaviour and I couldn't help wondering if famous writers were like famous actors. I'd met a few of those and noticed that they seemed to *need* an audience: it was as if they only thought they existed if they could see themselves reflected in other people's eyeballs. Were authors the same? Or were they shy, retiring creatures who only came out to talk in public if they were forced to? I couldn't wait to find out.

As Graham and I went off to class at the end of assembly, I said to him, "I reckon we should volunteer."

Graham stopped and looked at me suspiciously. "I didn't realize you liked any of those writers."

"I don't. I just thought it might be fun."

"Fun?" Graham looked unconvinced. "An ability to write doesn't necessarily translate into an ability to perform," he said, flashing me one of his blink-and-you-miss-it grins. "Remember the poets?"

"How could I forget?" During Book Week we'd had to sit through a reading from the local poetry circle. Poet after poet had intoned dirge-like offerings in strange sing-song voices full of Meaning and Significance. It had been bum-numbingly boring and had gone on for what seemed like for ever. "It won't be like that," I said confidently. "I bet they'll all be really interesting. They're big names, aren't they? They've got to be good. We'll go to the library at break."

Graham and I spend a fair bit of time in the school library. It's not that we're book-obsessed, you understand. But in the winter – when the wind's whistling across the playing fields and howling around the building – it's nice and warm in there. And in the summer – when it's baking hot and you've forgotten your suncream and the bigger kids are hogging all the shade – it's nice and cool. Plus, you don't have to put up with the football-crazed maniacs who love to accidentally-on-purpose shoot the ball at the head of anyone who strays too close to their game. According to Graham, a library is the cradle of civilization. He likes the computers and the reference section. I like staring out of the window. You get a bird's-eye view from up there, so I can study the playground dramas and crises from a safe distance.

The library's usually pretty quiet, but today, as soon as we rounded the corner, we could hear an unfamiliar babble of chatter. It seemed that I wasn't the only one wanting to get up close to the visiting authors. The library was packed with would-be student ambassadors.

"Oh great," I said, my heart sinking. "Looks like we're too late."

But fortunately our frequent visits to the library put us at an advantage. When we cornered a slightly harassed-looking Mrs Woodward in general fiction she gave us a friendly smile.

"Gosh, it's busy in here today, isn't it?" she said. "Amazing what a bit of fame can do to people's enthusiasm for reading."

I came straight to the point. "Can we be student ambassadors?"

Mrs Woodward's smile broadened as she pushed her glasses to the end of her nose so she could examine us more closely. "I knew you two would volunteer! I took the liberty of putting your names at the top of the list – I thought I could rely on you both to be sensible. As you're such keen readers, I think that's only fair, don't you?"

*   *   *

So that was that. We were officially designated as student ambassadors at the Good Reads Festival. According to Mrs Woodward we'd only need to meet a few authors and make the odd cup of tea. It wasn't going to be demanding. A nice, easy weekend, I thought.

I couldn't have been more wrong.

INVISIBLE MAN

AT precisely 7.45 a.m. on Saturday, Graham and I reported to the town hall. It was a vast Victorian building – all marble floors and oak panelling and massive rooms with high ceilings. The town council had deserted it for new, purpose-built offices years ago, and since then they'd rented it out for conferences and weddings and the occasional concert. It was the perfect venue for the Good Reads Festival.

Today was launch day. The whole thing was due to kick off at 11 a.m. with three simultaneous events: a celebrity chef would be doing a cooking demonstration in the café to promote his new book; there was a toddlers' storytime in the central library next door;

Then Viola Boulder walked in and everyone fell silent.

The first thing I noticed about her was that she was aptly named. She had a vast bosom and wide hips, but there was nothing soft about any of her curves – she looked about as warm and cuddly as a lump of granite. She wore big, round glasses and no make-up and her greying hair was permed into a whippy-ice-cream formation and sprayed with so much lacquer you'd probably have grazed your knuckles if you knocked against it.

Viola was one of those women my mum would have said had "natural authority" and I would call "plain bossy". The second she arrived she began calling out names and ticking them off on her clipboard, handing out official badges and schedules detailing everyone's tasks. Sue Woodward was down to set up tea and light refreshments for the authors. Graham and I were in charge of assembling their welcome packs.

Viola shooed a whole bunch of us down the corridor ahead of her.

"This is the writers' green room," she declared as we arrived at a set of heavy double doors. Pushing them open, she prodded us through one by one. "I want this room to be a haven of peace and tranquillity, and it will be strictly off limits to the General Public.

My authors can get focussed here before their events. Afterwards, they will come here to relax and unwind. No one without official identification is allowed in. Naturally I'll have security keeping an eye out, but you must remain constantly alert. If you see anyone who shouldn't be in here, you must inform me. I will not permit my authors to be troubled by over-eager fans."

Viola then went on to give us a serious talk about how we should all behave. According to her, writers were fragile, sensitive souls with easily crushable egos, who needed careful and delicate handling. One wrong word, one careless sentence, could stunt their creativity for weeks. I felt a weight of responsibility land heavily on my shoulders. Graham and I exchanged an apprehensive glance.

Once Viola had finished her speech, she directed me and Graham to a long folding table covered with piles of papers. Our first job was to assemble the welcome packs to hand out to the authors as they arrived. We were to man the table until 10.30 a.m. and then someone else would take over while we escorted Charlie Deadlock to his talk.

We got to work while Viola briefed the rest of the team. The packs consisted of a map of the town, hotel and restaurant details, the programme of events, official name badges – that kind of stuff. While Graham and I shoved papers into individually labelled cloth bags, we listened in on Viola's instructions. They sounded remarkably complicated, involving projectors, PowerPoint presentations and microphones. Tim, the technician, was clearly going to have an extremely busy weekend.

Once we'd finished assembling the packs, Graham and I had nothing to do but wait in the green room for the authors to arrive. People were coming and going through the double doors, bringing in urns and teapots and coffee machines and trays and trays of neatly cut sandwiches and home-made cakes to prevent any of the writers from starving to death. We sat behind our table, out of everyone's way. Graham had his nose in a book and I had one open on my lap, but I didn't read a word. I was too busy eavesdropping.

Sue Woodward was putting out cups and saucers and talking to a woman who I recognized as Gill from the central library.

"Are you all set up for later?" asked Sue.

"For Basil Tamworth? Yes, we are. Some of the things he needs for his talk are a bit unusual, but it should be fun, I think. How about you?"

"I'm hoping to hear some of Charlie Deadlock's talk. Have you read his latest?" asked Sue.

"No, I'm ashamed to admit I haven't. I gather it's

very different from those Sam the Striker ones."

"Oh, utterly. Quite honestly, it's hard to believe it's written by the same man. Such a leap! From football to *The Spy Complex*? It's brilliant. You must read it. Nigella Churchill said it was 'a work of rare genius' in *The Times*."

"Really? She's usually so harsh!"

"I know." Sue's face crinkled with irritation. "She's written some withering reviews in the past. I'm surprised any author will still speak to her. I can't imagine why Viola invited her here."

"Too important to leave out, I suspect. She's very influential, isn't she? She could make or break a new festival like this."

I was intrigued. Nigella Churchill: the name rang a faint bell. I'd had a good look at the schedule, but I knew Graham would have it tattooed on his brain. Being Graham, he'd probably also done background research.

"Who's Nigella Churchill?" I whispered.

"She's a journalist. A children's book specialist. I believe she's introducing some of the events."

Sue was still talking. "It's interesting that Charlie should have done something so very different. I read somewhere that he had appalling writer's block after he finished the football series. Apparently he didn't pick up a pen for five years. Can you imagine? Then he comes up with something so gripping! I was up until 3 a.m. finishing it – I really couldn't put it down. It's extraordinary."

At that moment I was distracted by someone entering the sacred green room. There were loads of people coming and going at that point, and I don't suppose I'd have noticed him at all if he hadn't been trying so hard to be invisible. His head was down and he didn't meet anyone's eyes. He slipped through the doors sideways, barely moving them apart, and then slid along the wall with gliding steps. He was smallish, oldish and thin-nish, with brownish hair and darkish eyes, and carried a plastic supermarket bag full of dog-eared, yellowing typewritten paper. He looked completely uninterest-ing; I was gripped. I try to avoid attention myself, not because I'm shy but because I like watching people – and if you're doing that, you don't want them staring back at you. This man didn't look shy either. He was Up To Something.

I elbowed Graham in the ribs. "Look at him."
"Who?"
"*Him.*"
"What's so special about him?"
"Nothing. That's the point."
"What?"

"What's he doing in here?"

Graham's eyes narrowed and he said, "Oh, I see. He doesn't have an official badge, does he? I'd better inform Mrs Boulder."

Graham was off across the room before I could stop him. There was no chance now of seeing what the man was up to. So I stood up, thinking that maybe I could go and have a word with him, but I knocked against the flimsy table and, with a loud crash, the legs collapsed and all the carefully stuffed welcome packs slid to the floor. Everyone looked around. I half expected the man to bolt back out through the doors, but to my surprise he stepped over.

"Let me help," he said, grabbing papers and shoving them back into their bags.

"Thanks," I said, flushing with embarrassment. "Are you a volunteer or a writer or something? Only you haven't got a name badge."

He gave a strange smile. It was slightly creepy. "I'm an 'or something'," he said enigmatically.

He didn't get a chance to say more, because just then Viola crossed the green room like a runaway rock – heavy and impossible to avoid.

"Who," she demanded, "are you?"

"Oh, I'm no one," the man said. "I was looking for..."

and for older kids there was a talk by Charlie Deadlock, the football guy. After that, there was going to be a buffet lunch for the chef and a host of other writers who were going on to do events in the afternoon and evening.

Graham was grumpy – he'd have preferred to spend the day in front of his computer. But I was quite excited. All those different characters to watch? This was going to be good.

An army of volunteers, including Mrs Woodward ("Call me Sue – we're not in school now!") had already gathered in the entrance hall by the time we arrived. We recognized some of the kids but none of them were in our year so we muttered hi and that was it.

The caterers were offloading supplies for the buffet. The staff from the local bookshop were falling over themselves (and each other) unpacking boxes and piling books high on tables. Someone was brushing down a Winnie the Pooh outfit for the toddlers' events. Someone else was hastily sticking up posters of authors and their book jackets on every square millimetre of available wall – only she wasn't doing it very well, so they were peeling off and fluttering to the floor as soon as her back was turned. It was all noise and chatter and chaos, and I couldn't quite see how everything was going to get done on time.

Viola cut him off. "Then you have no right to be here. Out! Out! Out!"

Beaten, the man retreated, sliding back out through the double doors. Tutting loudly, Viola returned to her preparations, and Graham and I resurrected the collapsed table and tidied up the welcome packs. When I glanced back at the doors I saw they weren't quite closed. An eye was pressed to the gap.

Fear stroked a cold finger down my spine. The man was still out there. Standing. Watching. Who, or what, was he waiting for?

DEATH THREATS?

BY the time the first author arrived, the invisible man had gone. Viola had stationed a security guard outside the green room, so I guess he'd been scared off.

I'd expected Basil Tamworth to look like a farmer, given that he wrote so many stories about pigs – a healthy, outdoorsy type with ruddy cheeks, a tweed jacket and faded corduroy trousers held up with baler twine.

In actual fact he was very tall and thin with carefully slicked back blond hair and long, manicured fingers. He was immaculately dressed in a sharply tailored linen suit with a crisp cotton shirt, expensive-looking gold cufflinks and a silk tie. When I handed him his welcome pack he dangled it limply from his hand.

Another man had followed him in – a weedy, wimpy-looking individual whose eyes gleamed with a desperation to please.

I didn't recognize his face from the programme, so I asked politely, "And which writer are you?"

"Who, me?" he said nervously. "Oh no… I'm not an author. I'm Trevor Bakewell. I work for Basil's publisher. I'm here to lend moral support."

Basil looked like he could do with all the support he could get, although I wasn't convinced Trevor was the one to provide it.

Basil was astonishingly pale, which I assumed must be from days spent in front of a computer writing books. But then I saw his brow was beaded with sweat. He produced a large, white handkerchief from his breast pocket and dabbed his forehead with it. "Extraordinary thing," he said. "We just saw Farmer Biggins. He was driving a trailer full of Gloucester Old Spots."

"Did the festival arrange some sort of publicity stunt?" Trevor asked me. "They might have warned us. It gave Basil quite a turn."

"Oh, I don't know. Sorry…" I said. Other authors had started to arrive and were piling in behind the two men. Realizing that I was just a kid and wouldn't be much help, they moved off.

Graham and I were kept busy for the next half hour handing out welcome packs and directing authors to where Sue was handing out tea and cakes.

Muriel Black (wizard woman) was closely followed in by the celebrity chef. Katie Bell (LURVE) and Francisco Botticelli (dragon man) arrived at the same time. Pretty soon there was a bit of a party atmosphere in the room.

I suppose authors don't get out much: they certainly seemed to be making the most of the opportunity. They couldn't stop talking. A lot of them already knew each other: there were loud air kisses and cries of "Daaarling!" and "How *are* you?" and "I haven't seen you since Edinburgh!"

When Nigella Churchill arrived there was a distinct frosting of the atmosphere. She had long, dyed-blonde hair that needed its roots retouching, and her eyes were heavily made up. She was also displaying what Sue later described to Gill as "an inappropriate amount of cleavage".

Writers either smiled or scowled in her direction, presumably depending on whether she'd given them good or bad reviews. Nigella strutted over to Viola, piercing the parquet floor with her killer heels, and asked after Charlie. When Viola told her that he hadn't arrived yet, she fetched herself a coffee and surveyed the room as if she owned the place.

After sending several dark looks in Nigella's direction, Francisco Botticelli and Katie Bell settled themselves on the sofa nearest to me and Graham and, to my delight, began to have a fantastically good gossip.

"Congratulathons on the Vellum Prize," said Francisco. He spoke with an Italian accent and a slight lisp. "You muth be delighted."

"Congrats to you too, sweetie," replied Katie. "I think we're all here this weekend, aren't we? She seems to have invited the whole shortlist."

Francisco lowered his voice. The sofa springs groaned as he leant forward. "Including Zenith."

Katie Bell stifled a gasp of disgust. "I know! God alone knows why she couldn't just stick to singing. Why do a kids' book, for heaven's sake? Can you believe it's been shortlisted? I'm sure that book was ghost-written. It's a disgrace! An insult to every author in the country. I'll bet she can't even write her own name. You know, when I heard she was on the list I almost told them where to shove their prize."

"Me too. But she won't win. And ith all stitched up in any casthe. Did you see Nigella'th review of *The Thspy Complexth*?"

"I know. It makes you sick, doesn't it? She gave

Stupid Cupid a right roasting." Katie sighed. "Which hotel are you in, Francisco? Shall we meet up for a drink or something later? Charlie's here today too, isn't he? And Basil's over there with Muriel. We could all go for a meal."

"That would be magnifico. Let me sthee where I'm sthaying."

There was a rustle of paper as they opened their welcome packs. And then the cosy mood was completely shattered.

Francisco gasped and muttered, "I don't understhand…"

"What's this?" said Katie. Her voice was harsh. Shocked. Upset.

I turned around in my chair. Each of them was holding a yellowed sheet of paper. Someone had cut out letters from newspaper headlines and stuck them together to create a message.

BEWARE THE DRAGON'S BREATH! screamed Francisco's.

CUPID'S ARROW WILL STRIKE! shrieked Katie's.

Underneath the words were grotesque cartoons of each writer. Francisco – roasted alive. Katie – an arrow through her heart.

"Is this someone's idea of a joke?" Katie demanded from the room in general. At the sound of an author in

Obvious Distress, Viola came thundering to the rescue. She was as appalled by the poison-pen letters as the two writers were.

"Where were they?" she demanded, her voice trembling with fury.

"In our packs," they replied in unison.

All of a sudden, everyone was looking at me and Graham. Me and Graham, who had stuffed the packs. Me and Graham, who had handed them out. Me and Graham ... who didn't have a clue how the notes had got there.

FOUL PLAY!

WORSE was to come. Viola insisted on rifling through everyone else's welcome packs. The first few she checked were devoid of notes, and for a second, Graham and I breathed a sigh of relief. But then she checked Basil Tamworth's. THE BOAR WILL BE REVENGED! squealed the message in his pack, and underneath a lurid cartoon showed an over-large pig biting Basil's head off. Muriel Black's shrieked KILL THE WITCH! She was drawn pinned to a tree, a sharpened broomstick through her stomach.

Viola found three more messages in the packs that hadn't yet been given out. THERE WILL BE FOUL PLAY! roared Charlie Deadlock's.

RIDING FOR A FALL! whinnied Zenith's.

BLOODSUCKERS DESERVE TO DIE! howled Esmerelda Desiree's.

There were graphic illustrations of each writer lying murdered: Charlie Deadlock, squished under a giant football; Zenith, trampled by a horse; Esmerelda, drained by a vampire.

Viola fixed Graham and me with a look that might have killed if we hadn't been so sure of our innocence.

"*We* didn't put them in there!" I declared loudly. "Why would we do that?"

"I can assure you, Mrs Boulder, it wasn't us!" Graham's protestations of innocence were equally indignant.

The organizer continued to glare at us, and I think we would have been asked to leave the Good Reads Festival then and there if Sue Woodward hadn't abandoned her refreshments and come to our rescue. The mild-mannered, cardigan-wearing librarian was astonishingly firm when she told Viola, "Poppy and Graham are both mature and responsible students. I can guarantee that they had nothing whatsoever to do with this."

Viola scanned me and Graham from head to toe and back again with her X-ray vision before giving us the all clear. Then she nodded once, sniffed and ordered everyone back to their posts. Fortunately, the celebrity chef was having some sort of problem with his anchovies, so Viola bowled away to sort him out. Graham and I were officially off the hook. For the moment.

"How did they get in there?" I whispered to Graham. "We've been here the whole time! No one's been near this table but us."

"Maybe it was that man," Graham said. "The one without a badge. Did you see anything?"

"Well, he did help me put them back together when I knocked the table over. I suppose there's no one else it could be. But why?"

"No idea."

Graham and I sat quietly for a moment, thinking. I glanced around the room. "There are loads of writers here," I said. "Why target those ones in particular?"

"I suppose we have to ask ourselves what they have in common."

I considered the matter. Every single author that Sue had mentioned in assembly had received one of those notes. Which could only mean… "I know! They all write kids' books."

"Very true," said Graham slowly. "And there's something else that links them all…" He paused, his eyes glinting with smugness.

I elbowed him impatiently in the ribs. "Go on, tell me."

"They're all on the shortlist for this year's Vellum Prize."

"That's got to mean something, hasn't it?"

"It has," agreed Graham, nodding earnestly.

The only problem was, neither of us could work out what.

By now it was 9.45 a.m. The uncollected packs were still sitting – minus their death threats – on the table in front of us. I knew Esmerelda Desiree wasn't due to arrive until the next day, but the rest of them would be turning up soon.

"What time is Charlie Deadlock supposed to be here?" I asked Graham.

"His event starts at eleven o'clock. According to the information Viola supplied, he ought to be here at ten. She's asked every author to turn up at least an hour before."

At that moment, Viola came back in and told me, "The chef's run out of olive oil. Run and tell the ticket office to send someone out for more, pronto."

Leaving Graham in charge of the desk, I set off along the corridors of the town hall. I delivered the message without incident, but when I started back, something odd happened.

As I turned a corner I saw a man in a football strip.

For a second I thought Sam the Striker had escaped from the pages of his books, but then I got a grip and looked more closely. His kit was the same as the one Sam wore on all the book covers, and he was wearing a Sam the Striker mask.

Now, I knew for a fact that Viola had laid on Winnie the Pooh outfits for the toddlers' storytime session, and Basil Tamworth had mentioned something about seeing Farmer Biggins. If he'd behaved differently, I might have assumed that the Sam the Striker lookalike was someone from the festival, dressed up to advertise Charlie Deadlock's event. But there was something sneaky about him. He was moving furtively, as if he was Up To No Good, and the moment he saw me he ran. The whole episode only lasted a moment, but I found it unnerving.

I returned to the green room and sat back down next to Graham, but I didn't get a chance to say anything. Before I could open my mouth, Charlie Deadlock himself strode through the double doors.

And then a football was kicked so savagely at the window behind us that it smashed through the glass, hit Charlie Deadlock squarely between the eyes and knocked him clean off his feet.

NOSEBLEED

IF Trevor Bakewell hadn't come back from the toilet at precisely that moment, it would have been a lot nastier. Trevor was directly behind Charlie, so instead of his head smashing against the wall, it thumped into Trevor's chest. They both ended up, sprawling and winded, on the parquet floor.

The attack was so sudden and so startling that it was a good few minutes before any of the grown-ups thought to peer out of the window to see who'd kicked the ball, by which time he was long gone. Graham and I, on the other hand, had looked through the shattered glass pretty much instantly to see the man in the football strip running away, scarily fast, along the street.

We'd both felt the force of that ball whizzing over our heads, and Graham and I stared at each other, eyebrows raised. I could see that we were thinking the same thing: whoever he was, that man was dangerous.

The writers' green room – that haven of peace and tranquillity – was in total uproar. Viola was torn between incandescent fury and abject shame that such a thing could have happened to one of her precious authors. "It *hit* him!" she gasped incredulously. "It actually *hit* him! I can't believe it!"

Nigella Churchill was on her feet making loud, barbed remarks about "inadequate security" and "amateurish organization". For a second I thought the organizer might hit *her*, but instead Viola began shouting at her minions to call a doctor and bring tea and phone the police and get security. She helped Charlie up off the floor and practically carried him across to the nearest sofa, fussing over him like an outraged mother hen. Trevor Bakewell took himself off to the far corner, where he plonked himself down next to Basil and started wringing his hands uselessly and occasionally emitting a high-pitched, anxious whine. Nigella strode over on her killer heels and sat down beside Charlie, patting his hand sympathetically. Charlie himself had a nasty nosebleed but that was all. He was batting people away, slightly embarrassed about the attention.

"I'm fine," he kept saying. "Really... As soon as this bleeding stops I'll be fine. Please don't worry."

Luckily, Sue Woodward turned out to be good at first aid, so she got Charlie's nose sorted out pretty quickly. Viola pressed a cup of hot, sweet tea into his hands. By the time he'd finished it, the author seemed more baffled than hurt.

"I suppose it was kids, was it?" he asked no one in particular. "Playing football in the street. They were a little over-zealous! That was an unlucky shot, for me at any rate."

No one but me and Graham had seen the guy in the football strip. While we looked at each other, wondering if we should say anything, the rest of the grown-ups muttered things about "kids these days" and "lack of parental supervision" and "I blame the teachers". They all seemed to accept Charlie's theory without a thought.

But Viola frowned and said softly, *"There will be foul play..."* She fixed us with another of her X-ray looks and demanded, "What are you two not telling us? Spit it out."

Slowly, reluctantly and no doubt looking extremely guilty, we described the man we'd seen.

"His back was to us," I finished. "We didn't see his face. Only..."

"Yes?"

"Well, when I came back from the ticket office just now, I saw someone in the corridor who looked exactly like Sam the Striker. And he was wearing the same strip as the man who ran away."

There was a stunned silence, which was eventually broken by Charlie Deadlock giving a small laugh and saying, "I do have some very enthusiastic fans. I'm sure it was just an accident."

"Yes," said Viola uncertainly. "Perhaps..." She looked helpless – as if she didn't quite know what to do next – and I could hardly blame her. It was all pretty weird.

Charlie brought her back to speed. "It's nearly half ten," he pointed out. "People will be starting to arrive soon. Could someone show me to my venue?"

"Are you sure you're up to it?" Sue asked. She glanced at Viola. "Perhaps you should cancel?"

Viola paled at the suggestion. Charlie's session had sold out. Turning people away from one of the very first events would be a public relations disaster.

When Charlie assured both women that he was fine and would go ahead, Viola nearly kissed him.

"I might just look a bit odd, that's all," Charlie smiled bravely. "But I don't suppose anyone will even notice."

I was beginning to like Charlie. He was nice and

straightforward and didn't like making a fuss, which was more than could be said for Nigella Churchill.

"I just hope they're paying you danger money," she said acidly as she got to her feet.

Graham and I had originally been given the task of escorting Charlie to and from his venue. He was giving his talk in a large room on the first floor, so it wasn't exactly difficult to find. But what with the drama over the football and the nosebleed, Viola insisted on abandoning the celebrity chef to Sue Woodward's supervision and accompanying Charlie up the stairs herself. She bowled along on one side of him and Nigella clicked along on the other, pearls swinging, bosom bouncing.

As we trailed behind, I whispered to Graham, "I'm right, aren't I? I mean, the man in the corridor must have been the one we saw in the street..."

"I agree," said Graham. "The likelihood of there being two Sam the Striker lookalikes in the vicinity seems very slim."

"How much damage did he mean to do?" I wondered. "Could you kill someone with a football?"

"I'm sure that it's theoretically possible. If Trevor hadn't been behind Charlie he could well have banged his head hard enough to cause a mortal injury. It was an exceptional shot," said Graham. "His aim was perfect.

I wouldn't have thought anyone but a professional footballer could have managed it."

"A professional footballer," I repeated. "Like Sam the Striker?"

"Sam the Striker is a fictional character," Graham pointed out.

"I know. But it's weird, isn't it? Like he's stepped out of the book... But why on earth would he want to hurt Charlie?"

"I can't imagine," said Graham. "The whole thing is utterly bizarre."

I couldn't agree more.

During Charlie's event, Graham and I were stationed at the side of the hall in case we were needed to run errands or carry messages.

When Nigella introduced the author to his audience she showered him with so many compliments that he started to blush. She said *The Spy Complex* was a work of genius that ought to win every prize available. Seeing as Sue had said almost exactly the same, I decided to stick it at the top of my To Read list. By now I was quite looking forward to hearing Charlie talk about it, but when he finally spoke, it didn't even get a mention. It was odd. I mean, I liked Charlie, but I have to admit that unless you were a dead keen football fan most of his talk was pretty dull, involving a load of photos of famous strikers and perfect goals on which he'd based his books. Graham and I were both yawning by the time Nigella asked for questions from the audience.

Someone stuck their hand up and asked where he'd got the idea for *The Spy Complex*. Nigella repeated the question more loudly so that everyone in the audience could hear and then turned to Charlie for his reply.

Charlie smiled. "A famous author once said that writers don't have ideas, ideas have writers. That may sound strange but I understand what he means. Sometimes stories just come into your head from nowhere. It's as if they're floating around in the ether looking for someone to write them. That's what happened with *The Spy Complex*. I just got lucky."

Someone in the back row waved a hand in the air. My stomach flipped right over. It was the invisible man.

"Yes?" said Nigella. "What's your question?"

The invisible man cleared his throat and then said in a soft, slippery voice, "I know you had writer's block before you completed your last football book, yet you finished the series. I was wondering how you got over it."

The question seemed innocent enough, but his tone struck me as sinister – as if it was a veiled threat.

He seemed as tense as a coiled spring, full of a strange, silent menace.

Nigella didn't notice. Maybe I was imagining things. As before, she repeated the question and then turned to Charlie for his answer.

Charlie looked extremely uncomfortable. He rubbed the back of his neck as if it had suddenly stiffened up, and it was a few seconds before he said haltingly, "It's true I was blocked, but it wasn't until *after* I'd done the series. I wrote fifteen Sam the Striker books in total, and by the end I'd simply run out of steam. I dried up. Didn't write a word for five years. Then, thankfully, the idea for *The Spy Complex* came to me."

It wasn't my imagination, I was sure of it. Nice as he was, I'd have bet all my pocket money that Charlie Deadlock had something to hide.

MAX SPECTRE

BEFORE Charlie finished his event, the invisible man melted away. I didn't even see him go – he was there one minute, gone the next. Spooky.

After his talk, Charlie signed books for his fans. They queued up in a more or less orderly fashion, and Graham and I were kept busy writing their names on Post-it notes and sticking them on the front covers so that Charlie could write the dedications without getting the spelling wrong.

By now Charlie's nose had swollen up – close to it looked as though it was slowly spreading across his face. Whether he was in pain or just upset by the invisible man's question was hard to tell, but he seemed irritable. He smiled at his fans as he signed their books, but it was a brittle affair that didn't go all the way up to his eyes.

Viola had to dash off during the signing because the celebrity chef's portable stove had exploded in the middle of his cooking demonstration and he was apparently in floods of tears. Nigella Churchill, scenting a story, went with her. So when the last of the fans disappeared, it was down to Graham and me to escort Charlie back to the writers' green room.

We'd only got halfway there when Charlie realized he'd left his pen behind.

"I'll nip back for it," he said. "You go on ahead. I can find my way from here."

He ran back up the stairs two at a time. If Viola hadn't given us such strict instructions about sticking with our author at all times we'd probably have done what he said, but neither of us dared incur her wrath. Graham and I followed him.

He was a fast mover, so we hadn't caught up by the time he got back to the room. It was empty now; the chairs had been stacked, the lights switched off, the curtains opened. As we reached the door, we saw Charlie picking up his missing pen and stabbing it into his jacket pocket so hard I thought he might do himself another injury.

The reason for his fury was obvious: facing him across the room was the invisible man. I don't know which of them looked scarier.

Graham and I stayed in the corridor, pressing ourselves against the wall on either side of the door so we could hear what they were saying without being seen.

"I'm Max," said the invisible man in a tone of silky menace. "Max Spectre."

"I realize that." Charlie was icily controlled. "I just don't know quite what you expect from me. You were well paid, weren't you?"

"Yes. But I've written something new." There was a rustle as he held up his plastic bag. "It's really good. The best thing I've ever done."

"Well…" said Charlie tersely, "send it to Fletcher, Beaumont & Grimm."

"An unsolicited manuscript?" scoffed Max. He began to laugh – a sad, embittered sound. "They won't even look at it!"

"Yes, well… It's a tough business."

"Look, I just need a little help. A word in the right ear. An introduction to the right person. Please… That's all it will take." Charlie didn't answer and Max sounded suddenly desperate. "Please," he begged again. There was more rustling, as if Max was trying to thrust the bag into Charlie's hands. "Just read it."

"I'm sorry," sighed Charlie wearily. "There's nothing I can do. I'm not a publisher, Mr Spectre. Or a critic, for that matter."

Max was getting angry. "I could tell them, you know. Your fans. Or Nigella Churchill. It would make a nice story for her newspaper."

"Are you trying to blackmail me?" Charlie's voice was chilling. "Because if so, I warn you that it will have serious consequences. I believe you signed a contract? I hope you read it properly. There was a confidentiality clause, Mr Spectre. If you break that, you'll be sued to within an inch of your life. You'd better keep your mouth shut or you might find someone shutting it for you."

With that, Charlie turned on his heel and strode back across the room. Graham and I fled towards the stairs, desperately hoping he hadn't seen us. The nice, straightforward, softly spoken author had sounded dangerously angry. If he knew we'd heard every word, I didn't much rate our chances of survival.

ZENITH

"**WHAT'S** an unsolicited manuscript?" I asked Graham back in the green room. The buffet lunch was in full swing and we were temporarily off duty while we ate.

"I'm not entirely sure," he confessed. "Perhaps we could ask Mrs Woodward."

We sidled innocently over to the librarian and Graham said casually, "If you've written a book, how do you get it published?"

Sue swallowed a mouthful of sandwich and said, "Bitten by the bug, eh? Bit of a closet novelist, are you, Graham?"

Graham didn't answer but didn't need to. Assuming

that he had secret writing ambitions, Sue ploughed ahead with an explanation. "It's terribly difficult to get started. Most publishers won't look at anything unless it comes from an agent. It doesn't stop people sending their work in, of course, and unsolicited manuscripts just get put on the slush pile."

"The slush pile?"

"Yes – manuscripts get piled up in a corner of the office, and once in a while a reader sifts through them. I should imagine that ninety-nine per cent get binned. Sad, really."

"So you need to get an agent?"

"Yes … and that can be dreadfully hard too, I'm afraid. Most agents are deluged with material – they all have slush piles of their own."

"So if I understand you correctly," Graham said, "you can't get a publisher to look at your book unless an agent sends it in. But it's difficult to get an agent because they're all swamped with submissions?" Graham glanced at me. "It would be enough to make you desperate, wouldn't it?"

Sue smiled and patted him encouragingly. "Persistence, Graham, that's the key. I'm sure if you want it badly enough, you'll succeed."

At that moment the high-pitched squealing of several hundred girlie-girls exploded on the pavement outside the town hall and swept through the building like a tidal wave.

"Ah," said Viola, putting down her plate and prising herself out of her chair. "I believe Zenith has arrived."

I wish I could have photographed the expressions on everyone's faces as Viola left the room.

Sue's lip literally curled. "Of course, if you're a celebrity you can get away with writing any old tripe," she said to Graham. "There's always someone who'll publish it, more's the pity."

Katie Bell and Francisco Botticelli looked at each other, their eyes gleaming with undisguised malice.

Muriel Black's face twisted into a sarcastic grin and she said something to Basil, who frowned, rubbing his side as if he'd contracted sudden, painful indigestion. Nigella Churchill drew her lips into a sour pout. Trevor flushed scarlet and looked uncomfortable, as if he'd been forced to watch one of her pop videos while his gran was in the room. Varying intensities of dislike were written clearly across people's faces. The only person who seemed immune to emotion was Charlie Deadlock; his expression was totally neutral.

Katie said loudly, "I can't believe they've got a ghosted book on the shortlist, can you?"

Francisco replied, "Ith an inthult. What were the judgesth thinking of?"

They both turned to Charlie, who was standing right next to them. They were clearly expecting him to join in, but he didn't. He simply shrugged. "It's not the judges you should blame. The readers nominate their favourites, don't they? Zenith is a name. You can't fight celebrity." He smiled apologetically and walked off to refill his plate.

Interesting, I thought. Very interesting.

It took Zenith a while to fight her way through the crowd of paparazzi and young fans. By the time she'd got through the double doors to the green room – shortly followed by Viola and a pair of leather-clad, heavily moustached minders – she only had a couple of minutes before it was time to fight her way back through to her venue.

The moment I laid eyes on Zenith I was fascinated. Her minders and Viola were looking hot and stressed, but Zenith seemed completely cool and untroubled. All that plastic surgery had given her an oddly fixed, almost reptilian expression, so it was hard to tell what she was feeling. But she seemed to be basking in the attention like a contented crocodile under a sun-lamp.

Graham and I were on escort duty again, but we soon discovered it was impossible for us to lead the way. In the end we had to give the minders directions and then follow along in their wake as they cut a path through the squealing crowds.

Zenith's event was being held in the biggest room in the town hall. There were five hundred seats in there, and by the time we arrived, every single one seemed to be occupied by a little princess in a frilly dress and spangly tiara. There was so much pink in there that it gave off a sickly glow. Hideous.

According to our schedule, Graham and I didn't officially have anything to do until after the event, when we were supposed to be doing the thing with the Post-it notes again. Pinky-Pony books aren't really my thing, and I was going to suggest we give Zenith's event a miss. But then I spotted Max Spectre. He was gliding towards the front row, carrier bag in hand, looking oddly hopeful.

"Graham! It's him again!"

"I wonder what he's up to now?"

"Let's find out."

We squeezed down the side of the rows, elbowing small children aside, and got to the front just in time. Zenith was about to take her place on the stage, but before she could step up, Max Spectre grabbed her by the elbow.

"Sorry!" he said. "Sorry to disturb you!"

She turned around and gave him a dazzling smile.

Or at least she attempted to. Like I said, she didn't have a whole lot of movement in her face. "I'm doing autographs after the event. You'll have to wait."

"No … it's not that. I'm Max Spectre."

The attempted smile vanished. "Oh," she said coldly. "What do you want?"

"I've written this book." Max held up the bag and spoke hurriedly, desperate to get his words out before her minders moved in. "Could you put in a word with your publisher? It would make all the difference."

Zenith didn't answer him – she didn't need to. Her minders had appeared, moustaches twitching menacingly. One cracked his knuckles and, without a word, Max backed off, drifting down the aisle and out of the room.

"Do you think we ought to tell Viola?" I asked Graham.

"What could we possibly say? We don't know what's going on."

"Something is, though. Something weird."

"I agree. But seeing as we don't understand what it is, I don't see how we could explain it to Viola. Besides, Zenith has her own minders. I'm sure she'll be all right."

But she wasn't. Five minutes into her event – just as Nigella Churchill had finished her introduction and the excited clapping had finally died down – a loud whinny ripped through the air. It was the sound of a horse, screaming in terror, and was followed by the clattering of galloping hooves. I looked about frantically, fully expecting to see a racehorse charging down the aisle, flattening the little princesses. But there was nothing there. It took me a full minute to realize it was just a recording, broadcast at full volume through the loudspeakers. Yet there was nothing fake about the brown, smelly stuff that then came raining down from the ceiling.

In two seconds flat Zenith had disappeared under a heap of horse manure.

THE OLD BOAR

ZENITH didn't stay for her event. She'd been literally dumped on from a great height. After they'd dug her out – which took a while – she charged out of the town hall and back to the hotel, pushing pink princesses roughly aside and threatening to sue Viola Boulder and pretty much every other human being who'd ever dared to exist.

Back in the green room, news of the incident was greeted with loud guffaws from Katie Bell and Francisco Botticelli. Muriel Black laughed until she cried, and even Basil Tamworth allowed himself a good giggle.

Katie, Francisco and Muriel were scheduled to do an event together right after Zenith had finished.

Nigella Churchill was chairing a discussion on "Reality versus Fantasy in Teen Fiction".

Their event was supposed to be in the same place as Zenith's, but of course the stage was completely covered in horse manure, so Viola had to hastily sort out a different room. Basil Tamworth was doing a talk in the library next door and the other rooms in the town hall were taken up with various adults' creative writing workshops and a desperately serious poetry reading. The only one left was where Charlie had done his session in the morning. Leaving dozens of heroic volunteers shovelling manure into dustbins, Graham and I escorted the three authors upstairs. We helped put the chairs back out while Tim clipped microphones to the writers' chests.

"Do you think one of them might have been behind the assault?" Graham asked me quietly.

I looked over at Katie, Francisco and Muriel, who were still chuckling.

"I wish I'd seen her face!" laughed Katie.

"Me too," sniggered Muriel.

"It musth have been magnifico!"

"They probably dislike Zenith enough to want to drown her in manure," I replied. "But if they planned it as a joke, wouldn't they have come and watched it happen? I mean, that would be half the fun, wouldn't it? The anticipation? No... I don't think it was them."

"It must have required a great deal of effort to obtain that much manure and load it into the roof space without people noticing," said Graham.

"Not necessarily." I know all about manure supplies. That's what happens when your mum is a landscape gardener. "There's a stables just down the road. It would be dead easy to get hold of a few bags. And it was chaos in here this morning. Anyone could have done it, I reckon."

"Max Spectre?"

"Well, he certainly gets around without anyone noticing. He seems to be popping up all over the place, doesn't he? Next time we see him, we'll follow, OK?"

Graham didn't look too thrilled at the idea but nodded bravely.

"Max seems to be the only one who links everything together so far, doesn't he?" I said thoughtfully. "I mean, he could have put those notes in the packs. He's got some sort of problem with Charlie – and Zenith. He tried to get both of them to take that bag off him. I don't know why he's doing it, but I think Max is our man."

"Should we tell someone?" asked Graham.

I considered for a while. Nasty notes. A football in the face. Horse manure. It didn't exactly add up to

Grievous Bodily Harm. Not yet, anyway. "Maybe he's just got a warped sense of humour. I don't think he wants to actually kill anyone."

It seemed I was wrong.

Halfway through their event, when Katie, Muriel and Francisco were enjoying a vigorous debate about the merits of gritty reality versus flights of fancy, three things happened simultaneously.

A deafening roar – the kind a real dragon might make if it actually existed – was followed by a burst of flame behind Francisco's chair. It was just as well he was so short – if he'd been any taller it would have blasted his head off. At the same time, an arrow flew through the air, embedding itself deep into Katie's chair, just a hair's breadth from her neck. And a sharpened broomstick swooped down from the ceiling, thudding into the floorboards right between Muriel's legs, pinning her dress to the stage.

For a split second there was a terrible, shocked silence, then the audience erupted into panic, pushing back their chairs and running for the door. It was every man for himself. The flames vanished as suddenly as they'd appeared, but it was enough to trigger the sprinkler system. Everyone on stage and in the audience was doused with ice-cold water, including me and

Graham, which was horrible but did at least have the effect of halting the stampede. There must have been a hot line to the fire station, because then we could hear the distant scream of sirens.

Viola's staff had been well trained. They evacuated the town hall more or less smoothly, and soon we were all standing, dripping, in the car park while the fire brigade checked the building.

Nigella Churchill's mascara had run all down her face. She looked like a killer panda, cursing Viola and threatening to write a long and detailed article about the "gross inefficiency" and "poor management" of the festival. "Your reputation will be ruined," she spat. "You'll never be allowed near an author again."

Viola didn't attempt to defend herself. She held her chin up and looked straight ahead, but you could see in her eyes how upset she was. If a granite boulder could deflate like a beach ball, that's what she looked like. Saggy and beaten. Her festival was in shreds.

Then things got even worse.

Ear-splitting squeals came from several directions at once. For a moment I thought the pink princesses were back, but then I realized it was animal, not human. Was it a recording, like the horse's whinny and the dragon's roar? I looked around for the loudspeakers. Couldn't see any. Then I got a waft of pungent farmyard smell.

Suddenly, the air was thick with it. And a piglet shot past me. A real, live piglet. Followed by another. And another. There were dozens of them!

And then Basil Tamworth was staggering out of the library, tie askew, shirt rumpled, his sharply tailored suit newly printed with trotter marks.

He'd been trampled by a litter of Gloucester Old Spots.

KILLER PIGS

THE police turned up not long after the fire engines, and what with them and the pigs it was mayhem. We soon discovered that piglets can run extremely fast. Once the town hall was given the all clear, the firemen attempted to round them up but they proved uncatchable. The sow, meanwhile, was in Attack Mode. No one even attempted to tackle her. Then someone had the bright idea of scraping the remains of the celebrity chef's failed cooking demonstration into a bucket and putting that in the back of the trailer. Once they caught the whiff of food, the pigs trotted in eagerly two by two like animals escaping the flood.

By the time the pigs were safely banged up, Viola's

granite will had reasserted itself.

"We will not be defeated!" she declared. Under such an onslaught the British Blitz Spirit came out in force and her army of Plucky and Heroic volunteers gave her a rousing cheer. Then she put them to work. While the authors supported each other to the nearest pub, Graham and I spent the next hour helping to scrape pig poo off the library carpet. Not a pleasant experience.

But by the end of the afternoon everything was more or less restored to normal.

"Tomorrow is another day," promised Viola. "We will assemble as planned. I'll see you all at 9 a.m. sharp in the town hall."

She was truly remarkable. A great leader. I was surprised that no one saluted.

"It was awful," Sue Woodward told us later as she gave Graham and me a lift back to my house. Sue, along with Trevor, had been with Basil Tamworth when they'd encountered the pigs.

His event had been held in the central library. There was a large meeting room right at the back which had been set aside for Basil's talk. They'd walked in, shut the door behind them and come face to face with the Old Spots.

"How did they get in there?" I asked.

"That's the odd thing. Gill said they were delivered first thing this morning by someone dressed as Farmer Biggins."

I remembered Basil's shocked, white face when he'd first arrived in the green room. He'd said something about seeing his fictional farmer. What was going on?

Sue continued, "The man had a note from Viola saying that Basil had requested the pigs for his event. I suppose it must have been forged. That room opens on to the car park so he parked the trailer outside and left them there. The staff thought it was a bit unusual, but it all seemed official so they went along with it. Later, someone must have let them out and herded them into the meeting room. You saw for yourselves the mess they made."

"How did Basil come to be trampled?" I asked. "Why didn't you just back out again?"

"Poor Basil! He gets so nervous! He's terribly shy – public events are torture, really. That's why Trevor came along to hold his hand, not that he was any help. Basil's mind was on his talk, and he was halfway across the carpet before he saw the pigs. Then he sort of froze. The sow was at one end and the piglets were at the other. Somehow he managed to get right between them."

"And, as we know, it's extremely dangerous to come

between a mother and her young." Graham looked at me, and I knew we were both remembering a tigress who'd killed her keeper in a similar situation. Graham added, "Sheep will attack dogs that threaten their lambs. And I gather that pig bites are particularly unpleasant."

"Yes, I suppose it could have been a lot worse." Sue sighed. "Viola was furious. She said, 'You'd think he'd know how to deal with a few pigs after writing all those books!' But he just stood there, watching the sow charge at him."

"How did you get him away?"

"Chocolate biscuits. I'd brought a packet along for afterwards, you see. I pelted her with them and she was thrilled to bits. While she hoovered them up, Trevor and I got Basil out."

It made me laugh to think of Sue hurling chocolate biscuits like frisbees at a charging sow. I complimented her on her quick thinking.

She gave me a watery smile. "It was a terribly narrow escape. He might have been killed! Imagine that! As it is, I don't suppose the poor man will ever want to talk in public again."

"But who's doing all this? Who could hate a bunch of authors that much?"

"I can't imagine," said Sue, biting her lip. "And what's worse – I can't imagine what will happen next."

COLLATERAL DAMAGE

THE attacks on Zenith, Katie, Muriel and Francisco were the results of very clever booby traps triggered by timing devices, according to the evening news. Inspector Humphries told the reporter that they could have been set up well before the festival began. So while the police trawled through the records of who'd had access to the town hall during the last few weeks, Graham and I tried to figure out what on earth was going on.

It was Saturday night and my mum, Lili, had gone out to fetch a Chinese takeaway. I reckoned we had about half an hour, maximum, to do some serious research on the web before she came back. She'd missed the news, but if she found out we'd got ourselves involved with more Suspicious Goings-On it would mean the end of our careers as student ambassadors.

We knew that all the authors who'd been attacked wrote books for kids or teenagers. The other thing that linked them was the Vellum Prize, so we typed it into the search engine and were rewarded instantly with the list of shortlisted books.

Katie Bell – *Stupid Cupid*

Muriel Black – *Wizard Wheezes*

Francisco Botticelli – *Dragons and Demons*

Charlie Deadlock – *The Spy Complex*

Esmerelda Desiree – *The Vampiress of Venezia*

Basil Tamworth – *This Boar's Life*

Zenith – *Princess Peony and her Perfect Pony Petrushka*

"So the only one who hasn't been attacked is Esmerelda Desiree, but she's not doing her thing until tomorrow," I said.

"I just hope Mrs Boulder has taken adequate security measures," worried Graham. "I would have thought Esmerelda Desiree must be next on the attacker's list."

It turned out that the Vellum Prize was worth a lot of money – the winner would walk away with a cheque for £25,000.

"There would be the increased book sales too,"

Graham reminded me. "And as we know, money is number five on the US Motives for Murder list. So maybe one of the authors is trying to get rid of their rivals?"

"If that's the case, they've had a spectacular lack of success so far," sniffed Graham.

"There have been some pretty close shaves, though. And actually, any one of them could have arranged an attack on themselves so as to avoid suspicion."

"Or Esmerelda Desiree could be behind it."

"True," I agreed. "But that would be a bit obvious, wouldn't it?"

Graham looked thoughtful. "I suppose another motive might be jealousy of those seven writers. There would have been a great many books nominated by readers. They'd have been put on a longlist, and from that the readers and judges would select the shortlist. Seven books made it: many more didn't."

"So ... someone might be really cross at being left out? Let's have a look at the longlist, then."

When Graham found it I let out a long, slow whistle. There were over 100 books listed, and some of them were as long as Francisco Botticelli's.

"Do the judges have to read *all* of them?" I asked, amazed.

"I believe so, yes. And in a very short space of time, too."

"That would be enough to drive you bonkers, wouldn't it? You'd be practically walled in by books. Do you reckon one of the judges has gone demented?"

We scanned the list of titles and authors. No names leapt out as obvious suspects – none of them had been invited to the Good Reads Festival as far as we could see – but there was one thing that surprised both of us. Nigella Churchill turned out to be not only a judge … she was the chairperson.

"That means she'll have the casting vote," Graham explained. "There are five of them, look. If they don't agree on the winner, she'll be the one who decides."

"And she's been going mad over Charlie's new book, hasn't she? No wonder Katie and Francisco glared at her like that. They said something about it being a stitch-up. They must know that Charlie will win if Nigella has her way."

"I can see why Katie or Francisco may have wanted to attack Charlie, then. Yet it doesn't explain why they became victims themselves."

"No," I agreed. "And they've all been so shocked, haven't they? I can't really see any of them doing it. So who does that leave us with? Max is definitely suspicious. *Spectre* … it's an odd name. Do you think it's real?"

Graham considered. "It could well be a pseudonym. Many authors use them. The Brontë sisters were originally published under pen names, for example."

"But Max isn't a published writer."

"No…" Graham said thoughtfully. "And yet there was that strange conversation between him and Charlie Deadlock." He paused for a moment, then added, "You know, spectre is another word for ghost."

"Ghost?" I seized on the word with interest. "Katie said something about Zenith's book being ghost-written. What did she mean?"

"It's when another writer is paid to do the work. I gather that most celebrity autobiographies are written that way. They have the celebrity's name on the cover, but a different person entirely is responsible for the contents."

"That's like cheating!" I said crossly. "Does that mean Zenith might not have actually written her book?"

"It's perfectly possible," Graham agreed.

"And it got nominated for a prize! No wonder the others don't like her…" I thought for a moment. "So where does Max fit in? Zenith didn't recognize him, so I reckon they'd never met face to face. But she knew his name all right, didn't she? It wiped the smile off her face when he said who he was. Maybe he wrote the book for her."

"It seems a plausible assumption."

"And if it's true," I said slowly, "that might explain all that stuff with Charlie, too! Sue said he had writer's block *after* he'd completed the Sam the Striker series, and so did he. But Max said it was *before* he'd finished the last book. Suppose Max is right? Suppose he knows the truth? What if Charlie *did* get stuck? What would happen if you got stuck with a book? Do you get into trouble with your publisher? Is it like being late with your homework?"

"From what I've read, writers often have deadlines to meet. With a series like the Sam the Striker books, the publisher would have arranged events – signings, appearances, interviews, that kind of thing. They would have been booked months in advance. It would have been vital to have the book ready on time."

"So … if Charlie was blocked in the middle of a book, could he have paid Max to finish it for him?" I asked.

Graham looked thoughtful. "It certainly sounded as if the two of them had some sort of contractual agreement. That would help explain why he mentioned the confidentiality clause – if Max did finish writing it, clearly he's supposed to keep quiet about the fact."

"And now Max has written something else – something of his own – and he wants help to get it published." I frowned. "Charlie wasn't at all helpful about that, was he? And Zenith looked at Max as if he was something she'd trodden in. It might all be enough to make him a bit unhinged. Maybe he's written stuff for the others, too…"

"It's possible," Graham said. "And he may well be a little unbalanced. Yet his chief desire seems to be the publication of his manuscript. I don't see how attacking authors would help him achieve that objective."

We fell silent. I recognized signs of Deep Thought on Graham's face, so I didn't say anything more until he spoke again. "The thing that perplexes me," he said at last, "is that there doesn't seem to be a single consistent motive that unites all the different attacks. I suppose what we have to consider is the combined effect. That way, we might come nearer to discovering who's orchestrating it all."

"Well," I said, "the festival has been virtually destroyed. I can't imagine that Viola will want to organize another one." The glimmer of an idea flicked across my brain. "I wonder…"

"What?" asked Graham.

"Whoever's doing it… Is it really the authors they're after?"

"On today's evidence I'd have said yes, definitely," Graham told me.

"Suppose someone's using them to get to Viola? Has she got any enemies? Her festival's been sabotaged from the word go. Maybe it's her they're trying to hurt. It's like in a war when you bomb a military base or something and civilians get killed by accident. There's a name for it…"

"Collateral damage," Graham supplied helpfully.

"Yes – that's it. Maybe the authors are just being used. You know how we always look for Motive, Means and Opportunity? Well, maybe they're the Means."

We Googled "Viola Boulder" but couldn't find very much about her other than stuff related to the book festival. She'd given various interviews beforehand, but all she'd talked about were the visiting authors. She was also a member of the local choral society and helped out on alternate Mondays at a charity shop on the high street, but that was about it. She seemed to be a fine, upstanding member of the community. We couldn't find a single reason why anybody would want to sabotage the Good Reads Festival. Even so, I couldn't help feeling that Viola might be the real victim.

Mum arrived back at that point, so we shut the computer down quickly and jumped to our feet to help with the food. She crashed out on the sofa and switched on the TV while Graham and I took the bag into the kitchen and dished special chow mein and crispy beef onto plates.

"Nigella's been pretty poisonous to Viola, hasn't she?" I said, crunching on a prawn cracker.

Graham nodded. "Whoever's behind the whole thing has a very detailed knowledge of the authors' works, which would certainly be consistent with them being a children's book specialist."

"And those notes were cut out from headlines – I wonder if they were from her own newspaper? I reckon we're going to have to keep a close eye on Nigella Churchill. But if she's doing it to get to Viola, I can't see her seriously hurting anyone," I concluded. "She practically worships Charlie, for a start. Maybe those death threats were just that – threats. The attacks might just be stupid, sick jokes. I mean, no one's actually been seriously hurt, have they? Perhaps they weren't meant to be."

As I tucked into my Chinese, I felt pretty confident that there wasn't anything much to worry about – but I couldn't have been more wrong.

The very next day we had a corpse on our hands.

PRESS ATTACK!

WHEN Graham and I arrived at the town hall the following morning, the pavement outside was awash with pale-faced, moody-looking goths dressed in flowing black velvet, desperate to grab front-row seats for Esmerelda Desiree's event.

We squeezed through the massed vampire-lovers and into the town hall, where Viola was preparing her troops for the forthcoming day's action. We noticed that she'd heavily increased the festival's security – there were a good few extra guards looking macho in dark corners, as well as two uniformed police constables standing to attention in the entrance.

The original schedule had me and Graham down

for helping out with the glueing and sticking at the make-your-own-pop-up-book event in the library. After that we were supposed to assist with crowd control at Esmerelda's signing. But after yesterday's catastrophes, it seemed that Nigella Churchill had made a few phone calls. The Good Reads Festival was now the object of intense interest to every journalist in the country. Viola had been forced to organize an emergency press conference, and Graham and I were reassigned to handing out tea and biscuits to the mob of reporters and photographers.

When they interviewed Viola, barking out questions as she sat rock solid on the stage, she looked cool, calm and collected. I could tell from her neck and shoulders that she was tense, but she spoke clearly and concisely and refused point-blank to speculate about who was behind "what I can only assume to be malicious practical jokes perpetrated on some of my authors".

There wasn't really much else she could tell them: she just kept repeating that no, she didn't know who was responsible and yes, she had taken every precaution to ensure that no further unpleasantness would occur. The police had been through the building with a fine-toothed comb and hadn't found any further booby traps. I have to say that most of the journalists looked a little disappointed.

The conference lasted about half an hour and was followed by a photocall. Every newspaper in the country seemed to want a picture of swollen-nosed Charlie Deadlock and poor bruised Basil Tamworth, the imprint of a trotter showing up nicely purple on his right cheek. They were less interested in Katie, Muriel and Francisco, who didn't have any actual wounds to display. Basil and Charlie obliged, smiling awkwardly on the town hall steps and looking slightly embarrassed. But the clicking and flashing of dozens of cameras drew the now manure-free and immaculately groomed Zenith out of the hotel like a moth to a flame. She strutted her stuff, posing and pouting, her lizard lips fixed in a broad, reptilian grin.

When the photographers had finished, the authors returned to the green room. They were all running creative writing sessions that day and needed to be thoroughly topped up with coffee and chocolate biscuits first. Zenith, on the other hand, was way too important to sully her hands with a workshop. Or maybe – if we were right about the ghost writing – she just didn't have a clue how to run one. She climbed into a violently pink limousine and returned to her country mansion, and I can't say anyone seemed even remotely sorry to see her go.

Following Viola's instructions religiously, we made

sure that our authors were warm and comfortable and well supplied with nourishment. No one was going to starve while we were there. And while we were busy topping up cups and opening more packets, we also managed a bit of eavesdropping.

Katie and Francisco were sitting together on a sofa. Muriel was curled in a nearby armchair. Opposite her, Charlie was apparently engrossed in the Sunday papers. Trevor was biting his fingernails whilst trying (and failing) to reassure Basil that pigs wouldn't invade his workshop sessions.

"I see that strange little man is hanging around again this morning," Katie said to Francisco. "The one with the carrier bag."

My ears pricked up at once. Graham and I glanced at each other and shuffled closer to the sofa.

"He told me hith name ith Maxth Spectre. Yesterday morning he athked if I'd look at hith manuthscript."

"He cornered me, too. I made the mistake of nipping to the ladies during Zenith's event. He even nobbled poor old Basil. There's one at every festival, isn't there? What did you tell him?"

"What I alwayth tell people. I'm justh a writer. I can't judge other peopleth work. I advithed him to find an agent or a publisher."

"Yes, me too. I gave him Fletcher, Beaumont &

Grimm's address and told him to send it there. He had a bit of a mad look in his eyes, though, didn't he? I found him rather alarming. Didn't he collar you too, Trevor?"

Trevor looked up, startled. "Yes, he did. I don't know what he thought *I* could do."

Katie shrugged. "I suppose he hoped you'd have some influence. You work for a publisher, after all."

"Only in the publicity department. And I'm so junior!" he whimpered. "It's not like anyone listens to me."

"The man's clearly desperate," sighed Basil, passing his handkerchief over his brow. "Do you think he's asked every author here?"

"He certainly asked me," Muriel Black spoke up.

"How about you?" Francisco called across to Charlie Deadlock.

Charlie looked up from his newspaper and his eyes narrowed just a fraction. It was a second or two before he replied and, when he did, he said flatly that he didn't know who on earth they were talking about. He'd never seen the man.

The conversation rolled on to other subjects and Charlie went back to his newspaper.

I looked around the room at the other authors chatting casually to each other. I was pretty sure none of them were hiding anything: in fact, I'd have bet my entire pocket money they hadn't laid eyes on Max Spectre before yesterday.

On the other hand, I was one hundred per cent certain that Charlie knew who he was – Graham and I had heard their conversation with our own ears, after all. So why was he so determined to deny it?

VAMPIRES

YESTERDAY the authors had arrived at the town hall under their own steam, but today Viola was taking special measures. It clearly hadn't escaped her notice that all the victims were children's writers. She was planning to be especially careful with Esmerelda Desiree.

Graham and I were despatched with Esmerelda's welcome pack across the road to the hotel where all the authors were staying. We, along with two security guards and a uniformed police constable, were then to escort her back to the town hall for her event.

As soon as we reached the hotel lobby, the receptionist put a call through to Esmerelda's room. Five minutes later she appeared at the top of the grand staircase ... and my jaw literally dropped.

It wasn't until I saw Esmerelda Desiree that I realized how deeply disappointing the other authors were. I mean, they'd all written brilliant books (with the possible exception of Zenith), but when you met them face to face they were nothing like their fictional creations. Sam the Striker, for example, was a superb footballer with the looks of a male model; Charlie Deadlock was fifty, fat and bald. Muriel Black didn't possess an ounce of magic, and Zenith looked more like a pantomime dame than a princess. Katie Bell's characters were young and beautiful with impeccable fashion sense; she was middle-aged, mousy and slightly scruffy. Francisco Botticelli wrote epic tales about evil sorcerers and noble knights, while he himself was small, slight and unimpressive: he'd probably fall over if he ever attempted to pick up a sword. And as for Basil Tamworth, the bruises on his face proved how incompetent he was at handling real, live pigs.

Esmerelda Desiree, on the other hand, was stunning. When she appeared, mine wasn't the only sharp intake of breath – gasps circulated around the lobby like a Mexican wave. She wasn't just young and beautiful, she embodied the essence of her book. *The Vampiress of Venezia* was about – you've guessed it –

the forbidden love and doomed romance of a teenage bloodsucker in sixteenth-century Venice. Esmerelda Desiree looked as if she'd stepped straight out of the pages of her book, like a queen of the night or an empress of the undead – gorgeously fascinating but totally deadly. She was as pale as her gothic fans outside, but whereas they looked simply ill, her skin shone like a pearl. Her hair was so black it had the metallic sheen of ravens' wings. Her lips and finger-nails were painted blood-red and she was wearing a dress you'd only expect to see on Oscars night – it should have looked completely over the top that early in the day, but somehow Esmerelda could get away with it. She was so beautiful, she could get away with anything.

She stood for a few moments, surveying the upturned faces in the lobby below. Then, with a per-fect sense of dramatic timing, she descended the stairs.

When we left the hotel, the fans outside dropped all pretence of moodiness: they clapped and screamed almost as loudly as the pink princesses had done for Zenith. Unlike Zenith, however, who'd basked in the attention (until the manure incident had dampened her spirits), Esmerelda Desiree seemed almost indifferent. Accepted it as her right. She was regal. Stately. The very essence of Cool. She walked forward, Graham and I trotting behind like a pair of poodles, and the crowd parted like the Red Sea.

We crossed the road without incident and were just about to enter the town hall when Max Spectre suddenly leapt from the shadows to block our way. One of the security guys moved forward to intercept him, but Esmerelda laid a pale, manicured hand on his arm and said in a deep, husky voice, "No. Let the man speak."

Max looked weary. Despairing. He held up his plastic bag and said, no doubt for the umpteenth time, "I've written this book. I need some help getting it published. I heard you—"

"I'm a little busy right now," Esmerelda interrupted, but then she gave him a gracious smile. "I have a reading to do. Maybe later."

Hope flared in Max's eyes. He'd clearly expected her to brush him off the way the others had. His sudden eagerness was pitiful. "You'll look at it?" he asked. "Really?"

Esmerelda was startled by the intensity of his response and took a step back, spiking the security guard's foot with her stiletto. He winced.

"Yes, well, see you..." Esmerelda said uncertainly.

By now, Viola had appeared and was coming down the town hall steps with the speed of an avalanche. Before Max could say anything, she bustled him out of the way. "I will not have my authors pestered," she barked. Meekly, we followed her in.

Esmerelda's event was in the same room as Zenith's had been the day before. The stage had been thoroughly scrubbed, but I thought I could detect a faint whiff of manure.

Tim, the technician, fixed a wire contraption around Esmerelda's neck, just above her collarbone. The mike nestled against her pearly white neck like a rather large cockroach.

"All set?" asked Viola.

"Absolutely," nodded Tim.

They both seemed quite wound up, but after yesterday's dramas it was hardly surprising. Tim sat down at the control desk and it was then that disaster struck. He went to pick up his coffee, but the cup slipped and hot liquid splashed over all the electronics.

Esmerelda's mike let out the most hideous screech, then crackled and died.

Tim looked as if he was going to be sick and all the colour drained from his face. When he said weakly that he didn't have a spare, Esmerelda replied graciously, "Don't worry. I was at drama school before I started writing. I know how to project my voice. I can manage without a mike."

Although Esmerelda seemed totally cool about it, I thought Viola was going to faint or have a heart attack or both. "No!" she gasped. "No!" The mike's demise seemed to have tipped her over the edge. "I can't bear it," she said in a cracked, despairing voice. "Not after all my hard work. That's it. I've had enough. I give up." She broke into loud sobs and Tim had to find Sue Woodward, who led her off to lie down in the green room.

Graham and I looked at each other uncomfortably, but we didn't have time to talk about Viola. Esmerelda's event was due to begin.

The doors opened, the goths poured in and, after the usual introduction by Nigella Churchill, Esmerelda Desiree started to talk. Once again, I was astounded. The other events I'd seen had been a bit dull, to be honest. Unless you were a mad-keen fan, none of the authors were exactly gripping. Esmerelda Desiree, however, was different. She was electrifying. Mesmerizing. When she read an extract from *The Vampiress of Venezia,* her audience hung on every word. I was spellbound.

Towards the end she asked for questions from the audience. There was the usual sort of stuff: what books did she like reading? Who was her favourite author? How long had it taken her to write the book? Where had she got the idea from? They'd all been asked that one. Katie, Muriel and Francisco had given virtually the same vaguely mystical answer as Charlie Deadlock – that stories just seemed to be Out There Waiting to Find an Author. Esmerelda, on the other hand, was very specific, describing in gripping detail a visit she'd made to Venice and how she'd walked the streets at night thinking up the plot.

Then a girl in a black cape asked if there was going to be a sequel.

Everyone in the room leant forward with eager anticipation.

Esmerelda didn't answer at once, clearly enjoying the moment. Then she said firmly, "No. I won't write a sequel."

A deep, disappointed sigh was expelled from every chest. The breeze rippled Esmerelda's raven hair.

"My publisher would love me to write another," she explained, "but I feel the book stands alone. I want to explore other subjects."

Nigella asked, "Are you working on something now?"

"Yes," breathed Esmerelda huskily. She cast down her eyes and added mysteriously, "But I'd rather not say what it is. All I will tell you is that it's a very different novel from *The Vampiress of Venezia*."

That seemed to bring the event nicely to an end. "I'm sure we're all looking forward to reading it," Nigella said smoothly. "Esmerelda Desiree, thank you."

"It's been a pleasure."

There was a long, loud, rapturous round of applause, and then Graham and I had to scarper to the book-signing table.

Apart from the hitch with the microphone, Esmerelda's event had passed entirely without incident. I commented on it to Graham as we walked along the line of goths handing out Post-it notes.

"It may well be because of the increased security measures," he replied. "The opportunities for an attacker will be extremely limited now."

"Mmm ... maybe. Or it could be because Esmerelda was nice to Max Spectre."

"What do you mean?"

"Well, now we know he talked to the others, too," I said. "What if he's been attacking people who won't help him?"

"Esmerelda Desiree may well be safe if that's the case," said Graham, frowning. "But Trevor had better take care. Max approached him, too, didn't he?"

I felt a sudden stab of anxiety for Basil's publicist. He wouldn't be covered by Viola's increased security measures – those were just for the authors. Was he

OK? I became more and more worried as the signing went on. It took ages. The queue of moody goths seemed to go on for ever, and they weren't content just to get their book signed and move off – they all had to have great long conversations with Esmerelda about life essence and the undead. I got quite twitchy.

Viola had told us to take Esmerelda along to the green room and restore her with light refreshments after her event, but by the time the last goth had reluctantly plucked himself away, Esmerelda said she was exhausted and wanted to lie down. We were under such strict instructions not to leave her alone that Graham and I, along with the security guards and the uniformed policeman, escorted her back over the road to her hotel. The whole time, I worried about Trevor and had this horrible gut feeling that something, somewhere was badly wrong.

We didn't dare abandon Esmerelda in the lobby, and en masse we followed her up the stairs to her room. I half thought we might all have to tuck her into bed.

It turned out I needn't have wasted my energy worrying about Max attacking Trevor.

Esmerelda Desiree put her key in the lock and pushed her door open. We saw Max Spectre, spread-eagled across the bed, staring up at the ceiling with cold, dead eyes. The pages of his manuscript were strewn over the floor. And his neck was punctured with two neat wounds.

When I saw those marks, my stomach turned right over. There wasn't a trace of blood on the sheets. It was as though every drop had been sucked out of him.

DEATH OF A GHOST

GRAHAM and I had met Inspector Humphries, the investigating officer, twice before. He wasn't thrilled when he found out that it was us who had discovered Max Spectre. When he arrived to examine the crime scene and saw me and Graham standing there, he muttered something about us being "the kiss of death", which I thought was a little unkind: it wasn't like we went out of our way to find dead bodies.

Inspector Humphries gave strict instructions that we were all to return to the town hall and stay there while forensics crawled over Esmerelda's hotel room looking for clues. Then, when he had finished his own examination of the crime scene, he followed us over to talk to the children's authors, who had all been pulled out of their workshops and herded into the green room. The inspector looked as perplexed as Graham and I felt about the whole thing.

Wiping his glasses with a crumpled handkerchief, Inspector Humphries told us it was possible that Max Spectre had simply been in the wrong place at the wrong time. As far as he could see, Max had gone to the hotel to leave the manuscript for Esmerelda to read. Someone had been lurking in her room and had killed him with a single blow to the head the second he'd walked through the door. The puncture "wounds" had been done with a felt pen purely for effect – that's why there hadn't been any blood. For some reason that struck me as odd, but I couldn't put my finger on why.

"Are you suggesting that I was the intended victim?" Esmerelda's voice sliced through the tense atmosphere in the green room like a knife. "Am I still in danger, Inspector? Do you think the killer will try again?"

Inspector Humphries surveyed his audience, then cleared his throat dramatically. "I believe every author here is a potential target. It was pure chance that none of yesterday's incidents ended in death."

There was a collective gasp of horror. Katie and Francisco paled and clasped each other by the hand.

Muriel Black drew her legs up and curled into a tight ball in her armchair. Basil Tamworth pressed a handkerchief to his mouth. Charlie Deadlock sat biting his trembling lip. Trevor looked like he was going to faint. Nigella sharpened her pencil and began scribbling in her notebook. Viola was weeping buckets of despairing tears and Sue sat beside her looking distracted, patting her half-heartedly on the back.

Esmerelda, on the other hand, responded in a very interesting manner. She put a hand to her heart and her eyes widened as if she was experiencing a blast of pure terror. She appeared to be in shock – she was doing all the right expressions, making all the right gestures, giving a very good impression of someone who had narrowly escaped being murdered – and yet her eyes were sparkling with something that wasn't fear. Excitement? Satisfaction? I couldn't tell.

Inspector Humphries commandeered the upstairs room to interview each of the authors and festival staff separately, starting with Viola Boulder. Meanwhile, Graham and I handed out cups of hot, sweet tea to fortify the nervous writers – who sat either pretending to read the newspapers, or staring wildly into space. When we'd done the rounds with the chocolate biscuits, we sat in a corner and whispered to each other.

"I don't trust Esmerelda," I said. "I don't reckon

she's really shocked. She's acting the part."

"Are you sure?" asked Graham.

"Yes. Something to do with her eyes. She looks kind of pleased with herself."

"She has every right to. According to today's papers *The Vampiress of Venezia* has now sold more copies than *The Lord of the Rings*. She must be a multi-millionaire."

I took another sneaky look at the glamorous author. Graham could be right. Maybe she was just glowing with self-satisfaction. "Is that why her publisher is so keen for her to write a sequel?"

"It would make commercial sense. There must be a huge demand from the reading public for a second book. And after all, publishing is a business like any other. They want to make a profit."

"I wonder why she's so dead set against it, then?"

"Perhaps she has writer's block too," suggested Graham.

"She can't have. She said she was already working on something new." Thinking of unpublished books got me back on the subject of Max Spectre. "It's odd that Esmerelda was nice to Max, isn't it? All the others couldn't wait to get rid of him. And Katie said 'there's always one'. It sounds like they get approached by people like Max quite a lot."

I knew that I was missing something – a vital piece of jigsaw was lost, and without it I couldn't begin to make sense of the whole picture. Frustrated, I changed tack.

"Do you think the killer really meant to murder Esmerelda?"

"Inspector Humphries seemed to think so."

"It all feels a bit odd. Bashing someone over the head seems clumsy to me. And a felt tip? It's not exactly clever, is it? Not like the other attacks."

"You may be right. But the puncture 'wounds' would tie in with the note. As I recall, Esmerelda's said 'Bloodsuckers deserve to die'."

I wasn't so sure, but I dropped the subject for the time being. I couldn't put it into words, but I couldn't shake off the sensation that there was something not quite right about the way Max had died.

I didn't share this with Inspector Humphries, of course. I knew for a fact that he wouldn't be remotely interested in my gut instinct. So when he called me and Graham for our interviews, I kept my ideas pretty much to myself.

Graham's mum and dad were both working that day, so it was my mum who came to the town hall to be the Responsible Adult present at our interview. She was about as thrilled as Inspector Humphries that we'd got involved in another murder investigation.

"A *book festival*?" she demanded furiously as we trooped up the stairs. "You'd think *that* would be harmless enough. How on earth did you two manage to find a dead body at a *book festival*?"

Graham and I kept our accounts brief and to the point. It was only at the very end of the interview, when we'd all stood up to go, that I suddenly found the lost piece of jigsaw.

A uniformed PC came into the room clutching Max's manuscript in a see-through evidence bag. He slapped it down in front of Inspector Humphries. "You asked for this, sir?"

"Yes, thank you."

"No wonder the man couldn't find a publisher," sniffed the PC. "I read a bit of it. I'm no expert, but I reckon it's bloody awful."

My stomach lurched. I couldn't pull my eyes away from the bag on the table, which was crammed with fresh, bright white, neatly printed pages. I remembered the manuscript in Max's carrier bag: typewritten, dirty, dog-eared and yellowed with age.

I had no idea who'd written the manuscript that had been strewn over Esmerelda's carpet, but I was absolutely convinced it wasn't Max Spectre.

THE PEN IS MIGHTIER

I did tell Inspector Humphries about the manuscript, but he wasn't exactly impressed. He made a brief note of it and then we were dismissed: free to go.

Graham had to come home with us, and when we got back to the house Mum disappeared into the kitchen to start on supper. She was furious with both of us, which was hardly fair: it wasn't us who'd gone and bashed Max over the head. But I couldn't expend any energy worrying about Mum. Graham and I had to figure out what was going on.

"Whoever killed Max must have stolen his manuscript," I told Graham. "I'm positive that one wasn't his. But he definitely had the real one in his bag when he talked to Esmerelda. I saw it."

"Theft…" mused Graham. "Robbery is number two on the Motives for Murder list. The intriguing aspect is that the manuscript was swapped. I wonder who would do that?"

"I suppose any of the authors could have," I said. "All apart from Esmerelda. We were with her the whole time, there's no way she had anything to do with it. But there's still something odd about her…"

"The person who 'discovers' a body is very often the murderer," Graham pointed out.

"But she didn't leave our sight the whole time. She's the only one with a cast-iron alibi." I sighed. "How about Charlie? He didn't want Max spilling the beans, did he?" I remembered Graham's words about celebrity autobiographies being written by ghost writers, and suddenly a thought struck me. "Suppose Max's book was his own autobiography? It might have had all the details about him finishing the last Sam the Striker book. That would give Charlie a motive for nicking it, wouldn't it?"

"It would indeed. And Zenith might feel the same if we're correct about him writing her book, too."

"But she'd gone home by then," I objected. "Although she's rich enough – I suppose she could have paid someone else to do it."

"I'm not sure that author assassination would be consistent with her religious principles."

"That's true. And even if Zenith was responsible, we've still got the problem of how today's events fit in with yesterday's attacks." I paused to draw breath and then said, "I think we might be looking at two separate plots, don't you? With two separate culprits. Someone wanted to kill Max, and they set it up to look like Esmerelda was the target in order to confuse the police. Maybe someone completely different did all that stuff yesterday. And that would mean that Esmerelda's the only one who's got away without being attacked..."

"...which brings us back to the idea that she might be the perpetrator," said Graham, completing my sentence for me.

I thumped the arm of the sofa in frustration. "But she can't have done it, can she? The death threats, the football and all that – she wasn't even here."

"As far as we know."

"As far as we know," I echoed. I thought for a few moments and then said slowly, "Of course, she could have been here without anyone noticing... If she was dressed differently – without the make-up and the posh frock – she'd be another person entirely. If she was in jeans and had her hair up in some sort of hat, for example, nobody would recognize her..."

"That's very true. She seems to be a good actress. She freely admitted she'd been to drama school. We have no idea who she really is underneath the glitz and the glamour."

"But why would she want to kill the other authors?" I wondered. "Back to the Vellum Prize, do you think? Could anyone want to win it so badly that they'd murder their competitors?"

"It's worth a good deal of money," Graham replied. "Yet she's a bestselling author. You wouldn't have thought she'd need the money."

"It's about reputation too, though, isn't it? You win something like that and people look up to you. Maybe that matters to her. Maybe it matters more than anything…"

So that was that. We concluded that Charlie was definitely under suspicion for the murder of Max, but Esmerelda was somehow behind the attacks on the other authors. We didn't know how she'd managed it, but she was our number one suspect.

Then the local news came on and all our theories were smashed to smithereens.

Esmerelda Desiree had just been found dead in her hotel room. Stabbed in the neck with a fountain pen.

GO WEST!

THE news carried a long piece about Esmerelda Desiree and her glittering career. There were live pictures of the scenes outside the hotel where her body had been found. Goths had gathered with lighted candles in silent tribute to their heroine.

Graham and I watched the whole item with our mouths hanging open. There was clip after clip of Esmerelda on various sofas – it looked like she'd done every single chat show on every single TV station in every single country in the world. It would have been enough to make every other author sick with jealousy. Was that motive enough to kill her?

The feature ended with Nigella Churchill giving a

long, slightly weepy interview in which she said that the literary world had lost one of its brightest stars.

"I talked to her just this afternoon," said Nigella chokily. "I was fortunate enough to have been granted an exclusive interview. She told me about her forthcoming book, *Go West!*"

My ears pricked up at once. Beside me, Graham gave a sharp intake of breath. This was significant news.

"She refused to talk about that this morning," I murmured.

Graham nodded, his eyes glued to the TV.

"Was it a sequel to *The Vampiress of Venezia*?" asked the interviewer.

"No – it was an historical novel set in the American West. I was privileged to see the manuscript when I interviewed Esmerelda. I was only able to read the first few pages, but it was immediately obvious that she'd produced another bestseller. It's a tragic, tragic loss."

The interviewer murmured something dull and conventional and then moved briskly on to a different item. I leapt up.

"That has *got* to be Max's book!" I shrieked, punching the air. "I *knew* someone had nicked it!"

"So what are we saying? That Esmerelda somehow managed to steal Max's work and then got killed for it?"

"That's about the size of it. All we've got to do now is work out how. And why."

"And then we need to discover who killed her."

"No pressure, then," I said with a grin. "I suppose we ought to start with the Why. She's a mega bestseller. Why would she steal someone else's work? Unless..." I grabbed Graham by the arm. "Suppose she *didn't* write *The Vampiress of Venezia*? It's possible, isn't it?"

Graham's brows contracted in a tight frown but I pressed on.

"Think about it, Graham. Esmerelda has stood out from the very beginning. All the others are nothing like their books, yet there she is – looking like a walking, talking vampire. The perfect package. *Too* perfect. I should have been suspicious about her right from the start. I bet she can't write a word. That would explain why she was so reluctant to produce a sequel."

"We have to consider two things," said Graham slowly. "Firstly, the manuscript that appeared in her bedroom. If Max didn't write it, who did? The same question applies to *The Vampiress of Venezia*. Who was the author of *that* if it wasn't Esmerelda Desiree?"

"Another ghost writer?"

"Perhaps."

"OK... So Esmerelda gets hold of Max's book. Although I don't see how she managed it." I shut my eyes, remembering the few sentences they'd exchanged on the town hall steps. She'd cut across him with an offer of help. Interrupted him. Why? What had he been saying? I struggled to retrieve Max's exact words, and at last they popped into my head. I spoke them out loud. *"I heard you..."*

Graham looked at me, puzzled. "Heard me what?"

"No ... that's what Max said to Esmerelda."

"What did he mean? Heard her on the radio? On TV?"

"It was more like he was going to say 'I heard you might be helpful', or 'I heard you were nice'. As if someone had told him to try asking her. She cut him off before he could say any more."

"So someone may have pointed him in her direction? Someone who was helping her get hold of the manuscript, maybe? That would suggest she was working with an accomplice."

"Who? Another author? Charlie? Could he be involved?"

"I've no idea."

We sat in silence, racking our brains. We were pretty sure Charlie would have wanted Max out of the way, but had he wanted Esmerelda dead too? Had he been her accomplice, then turned against her?

Unexpectedly, the television news gave us a

completely different answer. The programme was just finishing with a summary of the headlines. It reported the very latest on Esmerelda's death, and her publisher was giving a short interview. The name of his company appeared beneath him on the screen.

Fletcher, Beaumont & Grimm.

FLETCHER, BEAUMONT & GRIMM

MUM was still clattering around in the kitchen, but I could tell from the familiar rattle and bang that tea was fast approaching. We didn't have much time left to work things out.

I'd heard the name Fletcher, Beaumont & Grimm before – not once, but twice. Charlie had told Max to contact them. Katie had given him their address. And now their name was plastered across the TV screen in big, block capitals.

"Our association with Esmerelda goes back some years," the man from Fletcher, Beaumont & Grimm told the reporter. "She had a holiday job here when she was still at college. I like to think that was what inspired her to take up the pen herself. She was a great talent. She'll be sadly missed."

"Wow!" I said, turning to Graham the moment the news had finished. "Things are really starting to fall into place now, aren't they? Do you reckon Fletcher, Beaumont & Grimm had one of those – what did Sue call it? – slush piles?"

"I would have thought it was an absolute certainty."

"And Esmerelda worked there? So maybe *The Vampiress* wasn't ghost-written. Maybe she nicked it."

"But surely its author would have objected?"

"Not if she'd done away with them."

We quickly switched on the computer and trawled frantically through the web looking for something, anything that would help. It wasn't long before Graham had tracked down a tiny snippet of information on a newspaper website. It was one of those news-in-brief bits that you find tucked into a corner of the page, but it made sense of the whole confusing puzzle. It was dated three years ago and reported that a man had collapsed on the pavement outside the London offices of Fletcher, Beaumont & Grimm. It said he'd died of natural causes.

"I bet he didn't," I growled. "It's too much of a coincidence. Maybe he'd been visiting the offices. I bet he had a manuscript too – I bet it was *The Vampiress of Venezia.* The dates would be right. Esmerelda must have stolen it, then killed him. Find out some more, Graham."

But Graham couldn't track down anything else about him. We couldn't even discover his name. So we were left trying to fit all the pieces together, filling the gaps with wild flights of fantasy that would have made Francisco Botticelli proud.

Tea was a silent meal – Graham and I were in deep thought and Mum was still sulking big time. When it was over, she took herself into the garden to check on her cuttings, leaving me and Graham to load the dishwasher. It was then that I suddenly had one of those blinding flashes of inspiration. There was only one solution – one person – that tied every last little loose end together. The plate I was holding slid through my hands and cracked into pieces on the floor.

"We've been struggling with motives from the very beginning, haven't we?" I said to Graham. "None of them made much sense. I mean, Charlie may have wanted Max out of the way, but why kill Esmerelda? Esmerelda could have had Max murdered, but she wouldn't commit suicide with a fountain pen. Katie or Francisco or Muriel might have dumped manure on Zenith, but they wouldn't have attacked themselves. Who'd have it in for a bunch of authors anyway? It doesn't make any sense. But suppose someone was after just one author?"

"Esmerelda?"

"Yes. If that guy they found on the pavement *was* murdered by her… If he had friends or relatives who worked out what had happened… It's the only thing that makes sense. Revenge, Graham. That's what's behind it all. The whole book festival was a set up. Those death threats must have been put in the bags before we arrived. The attacks … that business with the pigs … we kept saying how well organized it was. There's only one person who could possibly have orchestrated it all." I grabbed Graham by both shoulders. "Viola Boulder."

"Viola Boulder?" Graham echoed incredulously. He looked at me as if I'd gone stark, staring mad.

I bent down to pick up the pieces of smashed plate, wrapping them in an old newspaper and shoving them impatiently in the bin. If I couldn't persuade Graham that my theory was right, how on earth was I going to convince Inspector Humphries?

"Think about it," I said earnestly. "She'd never organized a festival before. Why start now? The whole thing was a trap to get Esmerelda down here. Esmerelda was *meant* to die. The letters, the other attacks – all those were just a smokescreen."

"But Viola was outraged about Charlie and the football," protested Graham. "Don't you remember?"

I did. I could recall her exact words. "It *hit* him. It actually *hit* him." Her fury had been genuine, but maybe there was another way of looking at it. "Suppose the guy in the football strip was meant to *miss* Charlie and got him in the face by accident? That would explain why she was so angry."

Graham was unconvinced but I was well away. "The same with Basil Tamworth. Viola said something to Sue about how he should have been able to cope with a few pigs. It's like he wasn't supposed to get hurt. And Zenith wouldn't have actually drowned in that manure."

"Katie? Francisco? Muriel? Those things were potentially lethal."

"So how come they didn't do any harm? Those booby traps were brilliant. Do you really think that anyone clever enough to rig those up was going to miss? It must have been done deliberately."

"And where does Max fit in?"

"Inspector Humphries was right – he was killed by accident. Maybe he walked into that hotel room when Viola was rigging up a booby trap to kill Esmerelda, so he had to die. Then Viola had to go back and finish the job later. It was revenge, Graham. I reckon she's connected to the guy who died on the pavement. In fact, I'm absolutely sure of it."

"It's an enormous stretch of the imagination," Graham said doubtfully. "And we have no proof. If you telephone Inspector Humphries now you'll be accused of wasting police time."

As it turned out, I didn't need to. Inspector Humphries had come to the same conclusions I had. It was announced on the breakfast news the next day that Viola Boulder had been arrested. And when she'd been taken in for questioning she'd freely confessed to planning Esmerelda's murder.

VIOLA'S CONFESSION

THE news showed Viola being led up the steps of our local police station. At the top she'd turned and delivered a speech to the television cameras. She stood, proudly upright, and explained clearly and concisely that she'd had a brother called Sebastian Vincent – Tim the technician's father. He'd once written a book and given it to her to read.

"I knew at once that it was a work of genius," Viola said. "I advised him to send it to Fletcher, Beaumont & Grimm."

A month later he received a phone call asking him to come to London for a meeting, she explained.

"I don't know who he met or what happened at that

meeting, but when he was found dead and his manuscript was missing, I was certain he'd been murdered.

"Sebastian was on medication at the time," Viola continued. "It was only a minor complaint but it meant he wasn't allowed to drink. Yet the autopsy found traces of alcohol in his blood. The coroner assumed he'd simply forgotten – it was the Christmas party season, after all – but I knew him better than that.

"Sebastian simply wouldn't have made that kind of mistake. Someone spiked his drink. And as soon as *The Vampiress of Venezia* came out, I knew who the culprit was. Esmerelda Desiree was a leech. A bloodsucker. A thief and a murderess. She deserved to die. But let me state here and now that my plan went sadly awry. I was responsible for neither her death, nor that of Max Spectre."

"She's confessed to planning it, that's all," Graham pointed out to me as we waited for the bus to school. "She's denying that she actually carried out Esmerelda's murder."

"Yeah, well, it looks like Inspector Humphries doesn't believe her." The news item had said she'd been charged with both murders. Tim had been charged as an accessory and also with orchestrating the assaults on the other authors.

The bus pulled up and we didn't feel much like continuing the conversation in public. Then we had different lessons all morning, so it wasn't until lunch-time that we got a chance to discuss it more. We headed straight for the school library. Sue Woodward was about to close it for a few minutes while she went off to collect a sandwich, but she let me and Graham stay in there unsupervised.

"I'm not allowed to, strictly speaking," she smiled. "But I think I can trust you two not to go wild and wreck the joint.

We tucked ourselves into a corner.

I was pleased that my wild theory had proved right. But I was also starting to think there were too many questions still left unanswered.

"Satisfied now?" asked Graham.

I shook my head. "No. If Viola says she didn't do it, I believe her. She confessed to planning the whole thing – she seemed proud of it. Why not take the credit for the actual murder?"

The more I thought about it, the more wrong it felt. I sighed. "I don't get it… If Viola really did bash Max over the head, why would she mark his neck with a felt pen? What was the point of that? And who swapped the manuscripts? As for Esmerelda… Stabbed in her hotel room? It doesn't fit in with the rest of the plan, somehow. We're missing something."

"All the assaults were very public," mused Graham. "Staged, like pieces of theatre. It does seem strangely inconsistent that Esmerelda should have died in private."

"It does, doesn't it?" I thought back over everything I could remember about our time with Esmerelda, right from when we'd first seen her in the hotel. For some reason my mind stuck on an image of Tim sorting out her microphone. Tim, the son of Sebastian Vincent. Tim, who had just been charged as an accessory to two murders...

When the microphone had nestled against Esmerelda's pearly white skin it had reminded me of a cockroach. It occurred to me for the first time that her microphone had been an unusually large one – much bigger than the rest of the authors'. And he'd fixed it higher. The harness had fitted snugly around her neck, the mike's tip resting against her jugular vein. Then it hadn't worked because Tim spilt his coffee, and Viola had completely lost it. At the time, I'd assumed it was just the result of one too many disasters. Suppose I was wrong. What had she said? *I can't bear it. Not after all my hard work.*

Suddenly I felt sick. "Ohmigod, Graham! I think Esmerelda was supposed to die in front of us all!"

"What? How?"

"That microphone. It was another booby trap! I reckon there was something in there that would puncture the veins in her neck. Only Tim couldn't trigger it because he spilt his coffee on the control desk."

Graham's eyes widened. "You may well be right," he said. "That would be consistent with the other incidents."

"So Viola would have needed to come up with another plan. But before she could, *someone else* killed Esmerelda."

"What makes you so sure it wasn't Viola?"

"Because she'd have admitted it! She wasn't the least bit ashamed of planning the murder. She'd have been delighted to be the one to finish off Esmerelda."

"Yes, that's true," said Graham thoughtfully. "In which case, we still have two unsolved murders on our hands. We're right back to square one." There was a long pause and then he added, "What we have to consider is who benefits from both crimes."

"Well, I'm pretty sure Esmerelda nicked Max's book. But she can't have killed him."

"I think we may have been on the right track last night," mused Graham. "I believe we have to assume she was working with an accomplice. The question is, *who*?"

We looked up Esmerelda on the computer. Since

her murder had been announced, her book sales had trebled. *The Vampiress of Venezia* was already a world-wide bestseller. It must be worth a fortune. Which gave me something else to think about.

"Who gets her money now, Graham?" I asked.

"I have no idea. It would usually pass to her next of kin."

"She wasn't married, though, was she?"

"Not as far as I know. It certainly doesn't say anything about it on her official website."

We couldn't find anything helpful about her family on her official site. But – bless all those blogging goths – one of them had discovered that Esmerelda Desiree was a pseudonym. After a few minutes of trawling the web, we discovered that her real name was Rosie Bakewell.

"Bakewell?" I looked at Graham and my heart sank into my shoes. "Like Trevor Bakewell? They've got to be connected, haven't they?"

"The likelihood of it being a coincidence that they share the name is practically zero."

"So she's either Trevor's sister," I said slowly, "or she's his—"

"Wife." A familiar voice finished my sentence. It felt like being slapped with a cricket bat.

We turned. Trevor Bakewell was standing framed

in the door of the library, and he was looking neither nervous nor eager to please. He had a hardback copy of *Dragons and Demons* in his hand, and the expression in his eyes was positively murderous.

DEATH BY DRAGON

"WHAT are you doing here?" Graham asked nervously, looking around for Sue. Time was getting on; she was clearly having trouble tracking down that sandwich. "How did you get in?" Our school is usually pretty hot on security.

Trevor smiled. It wasn't a nice smile. "Your librarian is very industrious, isn't she? She persuaded all the authors to donate signed copies for the school, and I said I'd drop them in before I left town. The receptionist buzzed me through. It seems that my visit is rather fortuitous. You two were about to expose me, and I can't have that. Not now."

"So you did kill Max," I said flatly.

"Oh yes. Although I have to confess that part was Esmerelda's idea. I added the puncture marks: I thought it would be rather clever to mimic Viola's grand plan, and it's just as well I did. The police are convinced she was behind both murders. Very convenient for me."

"I can understand why you killed Max," I said, playing for time. "I know you were after his manuscript. But you'd got it. You'd succeeded. Why kill Esmerelda?"

Trevor looked pleased with himself. "It was all a matter of marketing in the end, darling. I was planning to pay a ghost writer to produce a sequel to *The Vampiress of Venezia*. It would have been a guaranteed bestseller – people were simply begging for it. As to the quality – it really wouldn't have mattered if it was second-rate. The brand was the important thing. But Esmerelda had begun to buckle under the pressure of being asked what she was doing next. She felt she had to come up with something herself. Frankly, she became a little delusional – she started believing she really was a writer!"

"That was her manuscript, then? The one on the floor?"

"I'm afraid so." Trevor winced in genuine pain. "It was terrible. I have to say, Max's book is good. Great, even. So now there will be another Esmerelda Desiree masterpiece on the shelves. Now she's dead, I'll have publishers falling over themselves to print it. I can rake in the money without worrying that Esmerelda will wreck everything."

"So you killed her for the money," I said. It was kind of disappointing.

"Well, not only the money. There was the problem of image, you see. When I found *The Vampiress of Venezia* on the slush pile, I could see right away it was a winner."

"*You* found it? I thought Esmerelda did."

"No. We were both working at Fletcher, Beaumont & Grimm – it's where we met – when I spotted it. It was simple enough to arrange a meeting with Sebastian Vincent when the offices were empty."

"But why didn't you just publish his book? Why did he need to die?"

"Because he looked awful! An old man in a tatty suit? He was bald; his teeth were dreadful; he was so shy that he could barely string a sentence together! You wouldn't want to see him on the breakfast news – he'd put you off your cornflakes. A writer like that just doesn't sell, darling. I knew that if that book was going to succeed, it needed the whole package – glitz, glamour, a stunning young author. It needed a touch of celebrity. It needed Esmerelda. And it worked. It worked spectacularly well."

"So why kill her?" I demanded.

Trevor sighed wearily as if I was extraordinarily stupid. "Because I knew she was going to ruin everything sooner or later. You see, the way she dressed, the way she looked – it was perfect for *The Vampiress of Venezia*. Then she got me to steal Max's book. What's worse, she told Nigella Churchill the storyline, so there was no going back. If I'd had my way, she'd never have given that interview." Trevor slapped his forehead in frustration and added scornfully, "*Go West!* What was she thinking? What was she planning to wear on the book tour? Some ghastly gingham frock? Cowboy boots? A ten-gallon hat?" He looked outraged. Then he remembered Graham and me, and a chill prickled my skin as I saw his eyes narrow. "Heavens! How I do run on! I must do something about you two before Sue gets back. Mmm, let me see. Time for an accident, I think. My goodness!" He ran his finger slowly along a line of books. "Your library is terribly well stocked. Shame the shelving is sub-standard. It's really not up to the job, is it?" After a last, calculating look, Trevor quickly grabbed the pole Sue used to open the top windows and rammed it under the nearest set of shelves, levering them over.

It turned out that Trevor wasn't as weedy as I'd thought. Before Graham and I could move, books were raining down on us. Volumes of epic fantasy thudded on my back as hard and as heavy as bricks. I put my arms up to protect myself, but it was no good. The corner of one book caught my eye, tearing the skin on my lid and temporarily blinding me. I tried to run, but I couldn't see. I slipped on the books, fell and knocked into Graham, sending him tumbling to the floor with me. We were both lying there, helpless, as Trevor upended another set of shelves: the reference section. Volumes of encyclopaedias. Dictionaries. The last fifty years' worth of *Guinness World Records*. We were trapped under the heap, buried from the neck down. Bruised. Bleeding.

And then Trevor was climbing over the pile towards us, the signed copy of *Dragons and Demons* in his hand.

"One more blow," he murmured thoughtfully. "One small tap just there where the skull is nice and thin. Yes, that should do it."

He raised the book high above my head. Graham yelled in fear and struggled to free himself, but his arms were pinned down with heavy volumes. I shut my eyes, waiting for the deathly blow.

But instead of a being struck by a fantasy tome, I was hit by a falling Trevor.

Sue had returned.

The noise of the cascading books had drowned out the squeaking of her shoes as she'd come in, and with astonishingly good aim she had flicked *Princess Peony and her Perfect Pony Petrushka* across the room and into the back of Trevor's head. It wasn't enough to do him any serious damage, but enough to unbalance him. He fell on to me and rolled sideways, crushing Graham, before scrambling quickly to his feet. Then he stood and faced Sue.

To our astonishment, the librarian straightened her cardigan and planted her feet squarely apart. Lowering her hips and sticking out her bum, she raised her hands in a martial-arts pose.

She looked so unthreatening, so completely undeadly, that Trevor laughed out loud. "You have got to be kidding."

"Try me," said Sue through gritted teeth.

Trevor took a step closer. "You know I'm going to have to kill you, too, don't you? This will be the greatest library tragedy since Alexandria burnt."

"Don't bet on it."

Buried under the book mountain, neither Graham nor I could lift a finger. And while I admired Sue's courage, I couldn't help feeling that a middle-aged librarian didn't stand much chance against a young man who'd already killed three people.

I was wrong.

Trevor took a second step forward. Big mistake.

With a piercing, warlike cry, Sue stepped sideways. Her left leg flicked up at Trevor's throat and the pointed toe of her shoe connected hard against his Adam's apple. Turning purple, Trevor clutched at his throat and gave a creaky wheeze. Sue followed up her advantage, chopping two sharp blows across his stomach with her hands. When he doubled up, she kicked him in the rear. He fell to the floor in a ball, coughing and choking.

While Trevor lay there, unable to get to his feet, Sue buzzed down to reception and asked them to phone the police. She then stood over him until Inspector Humphries arrived, giving him a swift kick every now and then when he attempted to move. In fact, I suspect she put in a few extra ones. I couldn't see much from where I was trapped, but I could hear the occasional muffled thud, followed by an "Ooof!" from Trevor, and Sue snapping, "Just look at what you've done. This is a library! That's no way to treat books, is it?"

There's not much to add, really. After Trevor had been arrested, it took a while for Sue to free us from the book pile. She was a little distressed when she discovered that we'd bled over some of the volumes, but she managed not to lose her temper over it. Graham and I were left with a few cuts and a lot of bruises but no lasting damage.

Trevor was put away for a very long time – he'd committed three murders in cold blood, so he received three consecutive life sentences. Viola and Tim were both charged with assault and the attempted murder of Esmerelda, but seeing as they hadn't actually succeeded they got off more lightly. It was just as well for them that Tim had spilt his coffee.

Sue Woodward, meanwhile, became a school celebrity. For the first few weeks after Trevor's arrest, the library was packed every lunchtime with people wanting to see her cool karate moves. It was only later on, when all the fuss had died down, that Graham and I managed to have a chat with her.

"Have you been to martial arts classes?" Graham finally managed to ask one quiet lunchtime.

"No," said Sue.

"Then how…?"

"I read a lot," she said with a shrug. "It's surprising how much you can learn from books."